**It had been too long since she had been kissed like this, Stacia thought, opening her mouth to accept the sweet slide of his tongue.**

She nipped at it with her teeth—human teeth—and at the edges of his lips, so full, so heated, so human.

*Human*, she reminded herself as a curl of heat ignited deep within her and slowly spread throughout her body, awakening the demon.

She battled back the vampire, wanting to bask in the delight of his attention. Savoring his honest but conflicted passion.

His gaze focused on her lips until he slowly lifted it upward and a puzzled look swept across his features. "Your eyes. They're blue now," he said.

The demon's eyes, she thought, surprised she had not been able to contain that aspect of the vampire. The even more confused look on his face confirmed that the normal brown of her eyes had returned.

"How—" he began.

"Do you really want to know?"

Dear Reader,

When Stacia first appeared on the vampire scene in *Death Calls*, I instantly fell in love with her as a character. On the outside Stacia was a brash and unrepentant vampiress who had no qualms about going after both Diana and Ryder to satisfy her sexual needs. But I knew that inside she was lonely and hungry for love.

It's taken me a while to find just the right person to give Stacia a happily-ever-after. Eventually it occurred to me that Stacia had already met just the man! Never mind that he was near death at the time and she was about to feed from him when pity made her help him live instead.

In *Kissed by a Vampire*, DEA agent Alex Garcia will come face-to-face with the sexy demon who has plagued his nights since his near-death experience. But Alex is unprepared for just how much Stacia will touch his heart and how badly he wants her to find the happiness she's been missing.

*Caridad Piñeiro*

## Chapter 1

The nightmares had sucked life from him for months.

Then they had stopped abruptly.

Tonight's bad dream was far worse. It sank its teeth deep and refused to let go.

Maybe it was wrong to call it a dream, Alex Garcia thought as he walked into a scene that was so vivid he could smell, taste and feel all that was around him.

The apartment he entered was dank and reeked of urine from the many squatters that had used the place for shelter. Only the chill of the winter night kept his discomfort to a tolerable level in the abandoned apartment. His cold sweat on the grip of his Glock turned the stock slippery. His gut tightened as he held his breath.

He was nervous.

Not a condition he was used to. He had grown accustomed to danger in his many years as a DEA agent. This mission was different.

Failure on this mission meant the possibility of death for hundreds of innocent civilians.

*Never again.*

He repeated the vow he had made after September 11, the one that had been the reason he had accepted this assignment.

He gripped the Glock tighter and moved farther into the apartment. He and his fellow Cuban Democratic Army member were supposed to pick up a stolen handheld smart-bomb delivery system that the CDA planned to use in the terrorist attack that he intended to prevent.

The weapon was not in the empty apartment as it should have been. As he turned to look at his partner, wondering if they had gone to the wrong location, another CDA member stepped from a back room and opened fire.

The force of the blow to his chest had him reeling backward. The pain was so intense he nearly blacked out from it. When a second blast immediately followed, ripping into his midsection, his knees buckled.

He fell back against the wall, slowly sinking to the ground in a sitting position, the body of the other CDA member sprawled beside him. The man's lifeless stare confirmed that he was dead, much as Alex expected to be shortly as his assailant trained his weapon on Alex's head for the coup de grâce.

The loud sounds of gunfire and an explosion outside the room distracted the shooter long enough for Alex to raise his weapon and fire.

With a surprised look, the armed man lowered his gun and stared at the blossoming trail of blood down the middle of his chest. It was the last thing he saw as he dropped to the ground, dead from a direct shot to the heart.

Alex had little time to ponder what to do next.

He was too badly wounded to move. Already he could feel the growing warmth of the blood soaking into his clothing and leaving a chill behind in his body. He was going to die there, alone and unable to do anything else to help stop the terrorist attack.

He had failed in his mission.

Outside the apartment all hell had broken loose judging from the noises reverberating in the winter night. The FBI must have moved in and the CDA was likely fighting back, determined to complete their plot.

A second later, the door to the apartment burst open, slamming against the wall.

His eyesight was fading, but he saw that a man had entered the room. He was holding something.

Someone.

He forced himself to focus and realized the man held Alex's ex-lover, but Diana wasn't moving. Blood covered the man's arms and hands as he embraced her.

Diana's blood. Too much of it.

Alex forced himself to take a painful breath,

attempting to speak. It managed to get the man's attention, and as his gaze wavered, Alex finally glimpsed the man's face.

Only it wasn't a man.

Shock gathered his senses, bringing Alex to painful alertness.

He had to protect Diana from whatever that was. He tried to raise his gun, only his body refused to cooperate. He couldn't move his arm. Couldn't even feel the Glock in his hand anymore as awareness fled his dying body.

A voice suddenly penetrated his fading consciousness.

They weren't alone in the room any longer.

He trained his attention on that voice—a woman's husky tones.

"This one's still alive."

Alex realized she was referring to him, not that he would be alive for much longer. That realization didn't bring fear for himself, but for those he had failed.

"Unlike your friend will be shortly," the woman added and motioned to the monster holding Diana in his arms.

"Leave," the demon commanded, pain evident in that one word, but the woman just laughed and sauntered over. She crouched before the demon and Diana.

Alex's hearing and vision were dimming quickly. Only a confused murmur of voices came to him, but then the woman shot upright and strode angrily across the room toward him.

Her bright, almost phosphorescent blue-green gaze locked with his, her fangs clearly visible. A vampire, he thought for the barest of moments.

Only, vampires weren't real.

What he was seeing had to be a product of his blood loss, he thought.

But as the woman leaned closer, there was no denying what stood before him. She stared at him hard and, for a moment, reverted to human form.

She was quite beautiful as a human, he thought, before the vampire returned and bent toward him. Sharp fangs grazed his neck as the warm kiss of her lips slipped across his skin, awakening ardor.

Bestowing passion that twisted together

with the pain in his body and soul as her fangs broke through his skin.

Alex shot up in bed, drenched with perspiration. Shaking from the reality of the waking nightmare and the desire that was always associated with it.

As he wiped his hands across his face, clearing the cold sweat of fear mixed with unwanted passion, he tried to scrub away the memories of the demon as well, but they refused to leave.

Refused to depart in much the way that the recurring memories of that winter night had not left him.

Alex cursed beneath his breath, hoping that he could muster enough control by the morning to pass his psychological review tomorrow. He had been itching to get back into the field for months. If the DEA psychologist picked up on the vibes from his nightmare, Alex was worried that the shrink wouldn't clear him for undercover duty.

Who could trust an agent in the field who worried that vampires roamed the darkness?

He had to get a grip, he told himself, lying back down and willing himself to go back to sleep. An untroubled sleep free of the night-mare of the failed mission and the monsters that haunted his nights.

But even as he was finally able to drift off, the vision of her face—both vampire and mortal—wove itself into his subconscious, leaving him to wonder if he maybe wasn't losing his sanity.

After nearly two thousand years of im-mortality, life had become predictably bor-ing. Possibly even depressing.

Not that being a vampire didn't have cer-tain benefits, Stacia considered, trying to convince herself that being a vampire elder rocked.

First, her age bestowed vast powers upon her. Incredible physical prowess and strength coupled with the ability to mentally control others, especially those vampires and hu-mans she had gifted with a bite or a taste of her blood.

Even better, her elder status also brought sexual pleasures and lust beyond anything she could have ever imagined.

So what if the price paid for those powers

by a shy virgin had been not only the loss of her innocence but her life?

She should revel in all that her elder powers could bring, Stacia thought as she perused the crowd passing before the veranda of her South Beach hotel. Excitement rose up at the thought of burying her teeth into the soft skin of a willing partner and drinking deeply. Maybe even creating a playmate to keep her company for a while.

Unfortunately, in her nearly two millennia of life, there had been not one partner worthy of offering a true vampire's embrace and the kind of existence that could follow.

What was worse, Stacia didn't believe it was even worth the challenge after so long.

It was why she had opted to come south since Manhattan had gotten extremely… bothersome lately.

All those wannabe human vampires with their goodness and love. Still trapped in the denial stage she had survived long ago. It was totally disgusting that so many of her men had succumbed to Cupid's senseless entreaty. Even Diego, nearly an elder by virtue of his own lengthy existence, had fallen for a mortal. A dying one at that.

At least Diego had had the sense to turn the human and bind her to him.

Not that it mattered to Stacia that Diego now had a lifelong companion. The human monogamy of her friends and all the melodrama that Manhattan seemed to offer lately had grown too tiresome.

She had needed a change of pace, and Miami had seemed like just the place to visit, especially after a disturbing and violent winter in New York City. The two cities couldn't be more disparate and Stacia welcomed that change.

She stepped from the veranda of the Park Central Hotel and out into the almost pleasant air of a South Beach spring night. Almost pleasant because the humidity was building even this early in the season, gathering strength for the hot and heavy days of summer that would be there in just over a month.

It had been nearly a century since she had done a Miami summer, Stacia recalled, gliding down Ocean Drive as dusk settled over the city. Flagler's railroad had brought the rich and wealthy down to the tropical climes, helping to create the metropolis that had provided a wonderful playground for her visit during the Roaring Twenties. Forty years later the diaspora of Cubans fleeing Castro would make their mark on the city and launch a new direction for Miami's growth.

*Ah, the Cubans.* Her mouth watered at the thought of something so deliciously different.

She hurried down Ocean Drive, hunger and need driving her toward Lincoln Road and the nightclub the hotel's concierge had recommended. As she reached the location, she noted the long line of humans waiting to enter and the muscle-bound bouncer guarding the door.

Smiling, she walked up to the man and sent him a mental command. With a dazed look, he obeyed, lifting the velvet rope to permit her to enter despite the grumbled complaints from those at the head of the line. With a sharp glance their way, Stacia silenced them with another blast of elder power.

Inside the club, dozens of couples moved to the beats spewing from the club's sound system. Speakers were mounted everywhere, creating not just a cacophony of noise, but an almost physical assault from the pounding music. Pings, chirps and shouts emanated from some rather avid electronic gaming in an adjacent room. An odd combination of noises, and while Stacia would have preferred a quieter venue, the push of vampire power confirmed to her that others of her kind were present.

Not many vampires, however. And not one of the vamps she sensed was as powerful as she was, Stacia thought as she threaded her way through the crowd. That was just as well. She didn't want to spend the night in a pissing contest with an elder worried about her moving in on his territory.

Plus, the presence of vampires in the club confirmed it was a good place to satisfy undead needs in a variety of ways.

Pleased, she continued onward, seeking her satisfaction for the night.

The Widget provided an odd combination of entertainment, from the dancing and nightlife in one section of the club to the electronic gaming and gadgets in another.

Of course, since certain sections of Miami had once dubbed themselves Silicon Beach, it only seemed natural that someone would one day meld that aspect of the city with those for which the city was more known— the beaches and nightclubs, Alex thought as he slipped from the low-slung seat of his customized Crossfire convertible.

Even though he was supposed to be on desk duty, Alex wanted to stay in touch with what was happening at his old haunts. A visit to the various clubs would help him be ready when he was cleared to return to his undercover assignment.

As those coming and going on foot passed by and the noises of activity within the club filtered out into the night, Alex hurried down an alley to a side door. It was guarded by a familiar face. The man smiled as he realized who it was.

"*Hola,* Alejandro. Good to see you."

The security guard embraced Alex heartily, clapping him on the back. He had the build of a sumo wrestler, was a good half foot taller than Alex's six feet and twice as broad as Alex across the shoulders and waist. He was also one of the drug dealers along the Ocean Drive strip and an informant Alex had relied on during many an investigation.

"Good to be alive, Pedro, unlike the guy who shot me," he said, playing the little game they always did. As far as most of the locals in South Beach knew, Alex was part of the underground that fed the sinful pleasures to be found as part of South Beach's nightlife. Only a select few knew he was an undercover agent.

With a playful jab to the other man's rotund middle, he freed himself from the bouncer's embrace and stepped through the door into the club.

The Widget was packed. Alex ducked and weaved through the throng, searching with keen eyes for signs of any illegal activities. As he passed through one section close to the video games, he caught sight of a familiar silhouette, but quickly lost sight of the woman among the crowd.

He peered over the people lingering close

to the dance floor, searching for another glimpse of her and thought he spotted her once again near the bar. As he elbowed his way past the bodies milling nearby, he confirmed that she stood at the bar, apparently waiting for service.

Her hair was short and dark, nearly seal-black, and cropped close to the elegant line of her neck. The dress she wore was lethally feminine, hugging her very generous curves and providing enticing glimpses of pale, creamy skin beneath all the black.

Something infinitely sexy about this woman called to him.

Dangerously sexy, he thought as his gut tightened with a need so intense his knees wavered.

His powerful reaction made him increase his pace toward her, eager to find out why she affected him so and why she seemed so familiar. But then the woman turned and smiled at someone beside her.

She wasn't alone.

He stopped dead in his tracks. He wasn't one to poach on another man's territory, only...

The woman's profile rang a powerful chord from him.

She seemed to sense his interest for she slowly dragged her gaze from the tall, well-built man next to her and transferred it to him. A moment of puzzlement narrowed her dark and exotic almond-shaped eyes, before a dazzling smile stole onto her lips.

Her smile appeared to be challenging him to come over. The pull of it was so strong that he stepped forward until she once again turned away to attend to her date.

Was she playing with him? he wondered for a moment before it came to him again that he knew her. He was certain of it, but Alex was at a loss to place the intriguing woman. He chalked it up to the brain fog he had experienced for months after the surgery he'd had to endure to repair his body's wounds. He blamed that lack of clarity for his failure to identify the alluring creature standing just yards away.

As the crowd shifted in front of him, blocking his view, he sidestepped a few people and then pushed forward, searching for her again.

Needing to see more of her.

But she was gone.

He dropped back into the crowd, questioning where she had gone. Wondering how it was that they were…connected. There was no other way to describe the reaction he'd had at the sight of her. However they knew each other, it had to have been something more than just a chance meeting.

Pity him for being unable to remember.

Her vamp radar detected the powerful thrum of interest.

She glanced away from the man next to her to survey the crowd for the origin of that sensation as they waited for the bartender to bring their drinks.

Her petite stature had her peering through the throng of bodies lingering nearby and moving on the dance floor. She peeked between the humans, then rose on tiptoe until her gaze collided with that of a handsome Latino.

Tall and well built, he had dark hair that was short on the side, longer up top and stylishly gelled into place. His olive skin lacked the tan of many in the establishment, but was creamy looking against the pale beige of his guayabera shirt.

He was intently staring her way, his deep green eyes narrowing to examine her as their gazes met and held. Her own was puzzled as she explored his features, trying to imagine why it was that he seemed familiar.

Puzzled that she couldn't remember someone so deliciously attractive.

She hadn't been in Miami in nearly a century, which meant that if they had met, it had to have been somewhere else.

His stare was so intent—so desirous— that it dragged a sexy smile to her face. A smile that dared him to come visit and explore whatever connection was happening between them.

When he returned that invitation with the determined glitter in his gaze, it roused desire, making her question how she could fail to remember him. Maybe Manhattan? She searched her memory, but her companion dipped his head close, dragging her attention back to him.

"The drinks are here," her dinner date

said, nuzzling the side of her face, the heat of his human state pulling her attention back to him.

She smiled, the handsome Latino man forgotten as the words from an old song—about loving who you're with if you can't have the one you love—played in her brain.

It didn't matter where she had seen the handsome Latino or why he was calling to her so strongly. For tonight, the man beside her would be the one to share her bed and be her meal. The attractive stranger would just have to wait until tomorrow.

The delay would only help tenderize him. Make him even more susceptible to her charms in the future.

After all, there would always be another tomorrow in her undead life.

## Chapter 2

The call came in the late afternoon on his office line, well after the DEA psychologist had cleared him for duty. The relief from the outcome of his visit to the shrink that morning was disturbed by the sound of his ex-colleague's troubled voice.

"Garcia. Heard you were back from leave," Dan McAnn said, striving for an upbeat tone but failing miserably.

"Back and ready to head undercover again."

"Good to hear," Dan said, but then an awkward pause filled the air.

Alex leaned forward and tightly gripped

the phone, his head hunched downward as he contemplated the reason for his old friend's call. Dan had retired a few years earlier after the stress of the job and family problems had created one too many issues at the office, including troubles with Dan hitting the bottle way more often than could be tolerated.

"Is everything okay, Dan? Do you need anything?" His inflection was conciliatory since Dan had been a good agent at one time and Alex had liked him on a personal level.

Another pause came on the line followed by a heartfelt sigh. "I'm okay. Got a great job as a security guard over on Star Island."

"Must be rough hobnobbing with the rich and famous," he teased, grateful to hear that his life seemed back on track.

"It's my kid, Alex. She's been missing for almost a week."

He reclined in his chair, now understanding the reason Dan was calling. "I guess you went to the police, but they don't want to do anything."

Dan let out an abrupt exhale. "You know that Andrea and I... She's been a problem child. Some drugs. Ran away right before I…retired."

Alex was well aware of the problems. Talk around the office had been that Dan's daughter had been the major reason he'd started drinking heavily and missing work. More than once Dan had run out of the office to deal with one of Andrea's scrapes with the law.

"Local law enforcement thinks she ran away again, and won't investigate," Alex surmised.

"Last time, Andrea was only gone for a couple of nights and she left a note about leaving. Took some things with her."

"And this time is different?" Alex prompted while reaching for a pad of paper and pen.

"She's been going to AA with me and we've both been sober for over a year. Andrea is really trying to keep her act together. But a friend asked her to go to a club—the Widget."

Alex had visited the nightclub last night. It was also where he had seen—and then lost sight of—that very fascinating woman.

"We've had our eye on the place for some time."

"Her friends say she met a man there. Went off with him into one of the private gaming rooms and never came back out."

"Can her friends provide a description of the man?"

When Dan replied affirmatively, Alex continued. "Can you give me their names and numbers?"

"You're willing to help me find Andrea?" Dan asked, surprised happiness lightening the timbre of his voice.

"I can't make any promises, but I'll ask around. See what I can find out. Check with the local LEOs, as well."

"Thank you, Alex. You can't imagine what this means to me."

But Alex could imagine what losing someone so special did mean. He had lost someone dear twice in his lifetime now and he had survived.

But barely.

And somewhere along the way, he had lost pieces of his heart and soul. It would be a long time before he opened himself up to more of that kind of heartbreak, he thought.

As he took down the information from Dan, it occurred to him that fate might just be finding ways for him to get his life moving forward once again.

First there had been that sexy woman from last night, and now he had a worthwhile case to investigate. Maybe a combination of both would help drive away the demons and nightmares that plagued him.

With renewed purpose, Alex dialed the number for the first name that Dan had given him.

From her oceanfront suite in the Park Central Hotel, Stacia peered past the edges of the thick blackout curtains she had asked the hotel to install. Considering that some of their patrons spent the night partying and the day sleeping, it wasn't such an unusual request.

But unlike the party animals nestled in their beds after their nightlong binges, she was up and about after only a short daytime rest, her elder powers giving her stamina beyond that of other vampires. It was a double-edged sword since what did one do with all that energy and wakefulness if one couldn't go out in the sun?

Especially the strong Miami sun. Stacia stayed at the window as long as she could before the strength of the afternoon rays on her skin became more than she could bear.

It had been another gorgeous late-spring day beyond the curtains. The cerulean of the ocean bright beneath a cloudless sky. A sweet ocean breeze rustling the deep green fronds of the palms through Lummus Park.

There had been hundreds of bodies on the beach, soaking up the daylight. She imagined the heat of their skin from the punishing rays. Imagined how such a sun-toasted body pressed to hers would take away the chill from her skin. Fantasized about sinking her teeth into that heated flesh and savoring sun-warmed blood.

A shiver of need danced through her at the thought, tightening her insides. Demanding that she find satisfaction. But the solar rays were still too strong for her to venture outside.

Satisfaction would have to come in some other way.

She strode to the small refrigerator tucked into the entertainment center in the room. Inside were the half a dozen or so blood bags she had obtained from the local hospital a few nights earlier. It hadn't taken much effort. With her elder power, she had slipped past hospital security with an implanted suggestion, found the blood bank and helped herself to some fresh O neg.

Removing the blood from the fridge, the chill of the plastic was a taunting reminder of how this snack was second best to those solar worshippers outside and of how cold she was.

Blood bag in hand, Stacia walked to the bathroom and eyed the tub. Decided a nice long soak would go a long way to eliminating the nip in her body. She filled the tub with water as hot as her undead flesh could stand and added a packet of bath salts that the hotel had left for guests. When the bath was ready, she returned to the room, slit open the top of the blood bag and poured a hefty portion into one of the wineglasses from the minibar. Some blood remained in the bag, and rather than waste it, Stacia quickly drained the container dry.

The energy of that small bit of blood surged through her body, awakening it.

Awakening needs of various kinds.

She sipped the blood in the glass as she strolled back to the claw-foot tub and placed her beverage on a small, filigreed stand. Whirls of steam rose from the water as Stacia slipped off her robe and then eased into the roomy tub.

The heat enveloped her, but it was a poor substitute for a lover's embrace. That would have to wait until tonight's encounter.

Maybe she would run across the handsome man from last night. The one who had seemed so interested in her. The intense look on his face had stayed with her long after she had lost sight of him in the crowd and then left the club.

For a few moments she let herself imagine how that intensity might feel directed toward her. How his long, lithe body, so much bigger than hers, would surround her and how he might lift her up against him with those muscled arms. Take her to her bed and fill her night with pleasure.

With a sigh, she reluctantly eased her arm out of the warmth of the water to grab her glass. Took a bracing gulp of the blood, which sent a wave of energy crashing through her insides.

Stacia gasped from the force of it, and as she sucked in a steadying breath, the scents from the baths slipped into her consciousness.

Eucalyptus.

Orange blossoms like those on the potted trees tucked into the niches of the walls in her family's bath.

Memories assailed her of those baths, driving away the pleasant daydream about her mystery man.

The scents recalled the times she had shared the baths with her family. With Hadrian, when she had turned him, centuries after she had lost her life and her innocence.

Lost both of them in those waters.

With her hand shaking from the blood's life force running through her veins, she brought the glass to her lips and took another deep gulp, nearly emptying it. She placed the drink back on the stand and eased beneath the water's edge, the temperature of the liquid feeling almost cool now that the vampire's heat surged through her body.

The desire stirred by the blood became unbearable, and as Stacia slipped her hand down between her thighs to satisfy that desire, the warm wetness and scents of the water transported her back to that fateful day.

*Rome, nearly 2,000 years earlier*

"Stop it, Cassius." Stacia giggled as she dodged her intended's amorous advances along their moonlit stroll. They had been walking for close to an hour, through the Forum and then back to her family's home near the Tiber.

Cassius grabbed hold of her hand and dragged her into the shadows by the door to the building holding the baths in her home. "The ceremony is tomorrow, beloved."

Tomorrow being the day her father would place her hand in Cassius's, turning over control of her to her intended along with the substantial dowry her father, a senator, was bestowing upon them to start their married life together.

Not that Stacia would be controlled.

At seventeen she was past the age when most of her friends had been married. Wiser than them, she thought as she snared Cassius's hand as he slipped it beneath the edge of her sleeveless tunic and pressed his body to hers. The obvious proof of his desire butted against the softness of her belly.

"Cassius," she warned again, but her beloved would not be dissuaded.

He inched closer and bent his head, bringing his lips to her neck. He dropped a line of kisses up to the shell of her ear where he whispered, "I have something I want to show you."

Stacia shivered as he tugged on her earlobe, desire awakening despite her better sense. There was something different about Cassius lately. In the past few weeks, ever since he had spent time with some new friends out in the country, he had been...

Sexier.

More demanding.

Infinitely darker, with a dangerous air he had not possessed before.

He must have sensed she was weakening, since he reached down, cupped her breast and unerringly found the tip, rotating it between his fingers and dragging a strangled moan from her.

"You are so beautiful. Let me show you how beautiful, my wife," he said huskily, the low tones of his voice strumming alive greater need within her.

"Wife now, is it?" she teased and pulled on a longish lock of his dark hair to draw him away.

"Tonight you are my wife. Tomorrow is only a matter of ceremony, no?" He smiled, his deep brown eyes glowing with a strange new light, the paleness of his skin a startling contrast to the darkness of his jet-black hair.

Had his skin always been that bloodless or was it an illusion from the moonlight? she wondered for a moment before he tightened his fingers on her breast, creating a sympathetic tug between her legs. The pull of desire was so intense she had to close her eyes against the strength of it, which just caused Cassius to chuckle.

"Do not deny yourself, Stacia. You are a woman of immense passion. I can show you great pleasure tonight. The kind of pleasure we will share forever, my wife."

Forever, she thought, imagining the life she would be starting with Cassius come the morning. Eager to begin a new phase since she had gotten bored with the mundane tasks of helping her mother run their household. It was long past time that she should have a home of her own and a husband to warm her bed.

"Show me," she said, and he chuckled once more, grasped her hand and led her into the baths.

Stacia dragged herself away from the painful memories of her once-beloved Cassius.

As something wet trickled down the side of her face, she brushed it away, but was surprised as she encountered the salt of her tears and not the bathwater.

Dashing away the tears, she rose from the bath and dressed quickly, needing to leave before the reminiscences brought more pain and disillusionment. She had no desire to let those emotions cloud the bright Miami days she had escaped Manhattan to enjoy.

As she dressed and shot one last look in the mirror, imagining how she might appear, another image pulled at her memory. The vision of her tall, handsome Latino—the one she had connected with briefly at the club the night before.

Yet again it occurred to her that there had been something familiar about his face, much as his expression had given away that there had been something recognizable about her. As she finally left her hotel room and escaped into the night, she tried time and again to place the man, but each attempt failed.

The identity of her mystery man would have to wait until later. It wasn't as if she didn't have an eternity of nights to find him, although she hoped it wouldn't take her too long.

Something about him whispered to her that he might be able to fill the nights that loomed before her, eternal and empty.

Predictably boring.

Recalling the determined glitter in his eyes, she decided that the handsome Latino would be anything but boring.

Because of that, Stacia hastened her pace, eager for the night to begin.

## Chapter 3

Alex handed the artist's sketch to Miranda, the final one of Andrea's friends he had to interview. The very last person who had seen Andrea entering the private area with the man they called "the Sheik." Miranda had agreed to meet him at one of the cafés along the Ocean Drive strip where they sat at an intimate table for two tucked beneath an umbrella.

Miranda took but a cursory glance at the sketch and immediately shoved the drawing back in Alex's direction. "This is the guy."

With shaky hands she reached into her

purse, pulled out a pack of cigarettes and offered him one.

He held up his hand. "No, thanks."

She lit up and took a deep drag, her actions skittish. Her eyes were hidden from him by the sunglasses she wore. She blew out a breath of smoke, and he watched it drift into the darkening Miami sky.

"You're sure Andrea was with this man at the Widget?" he pressed, just to confirm.

Miranda bent forward and perused the sketch again before nodding and taking another nervous drag from her cigarette.

"I'm sure. We had seen him there before. He always had a harem and lots of money, so we nicknamed him 'the Sheik.'"

"Do you know his real name?" Alex picked up his espresso cup and blew across its surface before taking a tentative sip.

Miranda glanced around, almost as if fearful to answer.

Alex tracked her gaze but observed nothing suspicious.

"Are you afraid, Miranda? Do you think—"

"He'll come get me?" Miranda took a long

pull on her cigarette before forcefully blowing out a plume of smoke.

"So, are you afraid?" he repeated when she delayed.

Miranda shrugged. "I don't plan on going back to the Widget. Ever."

"No one asked you to do that, Miranda. I just need you to tell me a little something more about that night and this man." Alex flipped the sketch around so Miranda could not avoid seeing it.

Another shrug came in answer, shifting the strap of the loose black tank top she wore. The shirt dipped to reveal the curves of her breasts and no bra.

Miranda pulled the strap back into place as she said, "We went. We saw. She conquered."

Alex raised an eyebrow. "*She,* as in Andrea?"

Miranda nodded. "Andrea had been intrigued by the Sheik more than the rest of us. That night she was determined to meet him, so she was dressed to kill. It seemed like it was her lucky night."

"Why's that?" Alex leaned toward her

so he could read the nuances in her body language. He wished she would remove her damned sunglasses so he could see her eyes.

Eyes could definitely tell you a hell of a lot more than words alone.

Amazingly she did as he had wished, tossing aside the sunglasses before dragging a hand through the long locks of her dark hair.

She had old eyes, he decided. Aged beyond her twentysomething years. A sure sign of a hard life, but given what he knew of Andrea's past, he supposed her friend's eyes mirrored that. Drugs and other problems had taken their toll.

"The Sheik was alone that night. Drinking at the bar all by his lonesome. Andrea jumped on the opportunity to meet him."

And to jump on him, Alex suspected but didn't say. "So they spent time together at the club?"

Miranda nodded. "Dancing. Drinking. After, he took her to the video-game area."

"You saw her there? In the video-game area?"

Another quick bob of Miranda's head confirmed it before she said, "For an hour or so. Then she went with him into the private rooms. We thought she was going to one of those luxury gaming digs that everyone was always talking about."

"And that was the last time you saw her? You didn't think to call or check on her the next day? Or the day after that?"

She winced at the condemnation in his voice, which he hadn't been able to control. Even if Andrea hadn't been Dan's daughter, it would have been hard not to question what kind of friends she had. Friends who had left her without a second thought, apparently, and who hadn't worried about what had happened to her until Andrea's father had started asking around.

"We figured she'd hit the jackpot. The Sheik was always a high roller. Handsome. He could get into the private rooms. Do you know how hard it is to get into that area?" she said, gripping the edges of the table as she leaned toward him to emphasize her point.

"I guess I'm going to find out," he said and rose. "Thanks for your help."

Miranda nodded, and Alex tossed some money on the table to cover their check.

He walked away and crossed the street to Lummus Park. The activity in its gardens and along the walkways had changed from the morning beachgoers to those who would be strolling along the strip to pick a place to eat before heading out to party later that night.

It was still too early for him to scope out the Widget, although he was eager to return there, and not just on account of his investigation into Andrea's disappearance.

The demon had come to him in his dreams once again, but she had been more mortal this time. Looking way too much like the woman he had seen last night. He didn't know if he should take that as an omen to avoid her because she'd be nothing but trouble.

Despite that bothersome possibility, she had awakened a different kind of need in his dreams—a desire to discover more about her. To find out why the demon who had been haunting him for months was suddenly pointing him in the direction of his mystery woman.

He popped open the doors on his Crossfire convertible, which was parked on the street across from the News Café where he had met Miranda.

With a quick glance at his watch, he slipped into the low-slung car, experiencing only a slight pull in his midsection in the area where he had been shot nearly a year earlier. He paused for a moment, pressing against the spot to tame the stitch in his muscles, and then lowered the top on the convertible. After a quick cruise up and down Ocean Drive to see who was out and about, he then headed back to his office to review his files and notes once again before returning to South Beach.

The problem with the DEA materials he had reviewed was that he didn't recall seeing anyone in their extensive databases and papers who matched the general description of the man Andrea's friends had dubbed "the Sheik." That could mean that the man wasn't as much of a player as Andrea and her friends had thought. But although the Sheik hadn't made the DEA's watch list, maybe the man had come to the attention of the local law-enforcement officers.

Which meant that it was time he arrange for a visit to the neighborhood police department and speak to those LEOs. Maybe the Sheik had crossed paths with them and they could provide some background information on the man and his associates.

But not tonight.

Tonight he had to scope out the clubs one more time.

He owed it to Dan to find the Sheik and hopefully Andrea.

He owed it to himself to find the mystery woman from his dreams. For too long he had lived without allowing himself the pleasure of a woman's company. First because of his heartache over losing his ex-lover, Diana, to her vampire lover and more recently because of his commitment to his work.

There had been a challenge in his mystery woman's eyes, almost daring him to come and play for a while. It reminded him of the demon in his dreams as she bent to taste his blood. Maybe accepting her dare would allow him a respite from the prison he had created for himself with his obligations to his job.

Alex decided to take up that challenge, if only for a short break from the duties he took so seriously. He knew his heartache would not be so easy to forget.

Stacia smoothed the slick bloodred fabric across the flat lines of her belly. The color was a shock against the paleness of her skin and the nearly ebony shade of her hair and eyes. The bright hue was unfamiliar. She usually favored black and leather.

The Miami humidity factored against the latter, and something about the locale had her tossing aside all the New York black. Appropriate since the reason for coming to Miami had been to exact a change in the tedium of her eternal life.

Satisfied with her appearance, Stacia left her room and exited hastily onto the veranda of the hotel.

The nighttime activity had picked up and dozens of people streamed by in front of the hotel. Dressed in their finery, they were like peacocks on display. She honed in on the energy of their life forces. Savored the differences she detected in their powers: young; not quite old; strong; stronger still.

This was no place for imperfection in this crowd.

A slightly familiar energy came near and she smiled, recognizing a man from the night before. While she had been trolling for last night's catch, she had implanted a suggestion in him to return to this spot since he hadn't been quite what she wanted but had possessed possibilities. Not as many possibilities as the other intriguing Cubano, but for now he would do.

The man approached. Tall and sleek. Broad shoulders covered in a jacket of expensive raw linen, creamy against the darker tones of his skin and hair. The man smiled as he took note of Stacia up on the veranda and slowed his pace.

He would be such a fine repast, Stacia thought, detecting the vibrant pulse of his life force. Imagining how she would sink her teeth into the long, elegant line of the stranger's neck.

Stacia strengthened the push of her elder power, calling to the man to come to her. As he neared, their gazes converged but something there sent a jolt through Stacia.

The man's eyes were so dark as to appear black, reminding her of Cassius's gaze, the deceiving, empty gaze that had stolen so much from her millennia ago.

Stacia released her control over him and he shook his head as if suddenly awakening.

He did an about-face and relief washed over her. Funny, really. There were few things that could scare an elder of her age and power, and yet...

She had her own demons.

Demons she had kept hidden for incredibly long to avoid displaying her weaknesses.

In a world as difficult as the vampire realm, any hint of debility made her vulnerable to attack. Something she had avoided successfully for centuries.

Until New York City.

Until the wannabe humans in that vampire underworld had reminded her of her one weakness. Of the single need she had kept buried deep within her for centuries.

To be loved once again.

Driving those thoughts away, Stacia slinked

down the steps of the hotel, intending to savor the coming of a Miami night.

She ambled across the street to Lummus Park, slowly making her way along the winding cement walkway that separated the gardens from the beach. The walkway was relatively quiet, although she passed a few couples meandering beneath the palms and sea-grape trees. An in-line skater whizzed past her, lithe leg muscles propelling him to his destination.

She admired his lean buttocks and broad upper body for only a moment before he skated out of sight.

Peering toward the ocean, the moonlight silvered the crests of the negligible waves washing against the shore. Illuminated the occasional human strolling along the Atlantic's edge. She considered grabbing a snack down along the oceanfront, but the possibility of a chase through the sand would be too much effort tonight. Maybe some other night when she had to release some excess energy and would actually welcome a challenging hunt.

Stacia continued until the end of the path and then crossed the street once more, all the time checking out the offerings, both human and not, in the restaurants along the strip. The food selections were varied, from the expected Cuban offerings to traditional Italian and an assortment of Asian-fusion choices.

She'd had her taste of Cuban last night. The murderous happenings in Manhattan before she had left had her swearing off Asian. That cuisine would remind her too much of the Kiang-shi vampire that had killed a number of the undead and nearly revealed their vampire underworld to the humans.

Italian possibly? she thought, noticing a fine-looking specimen lingering near one establishment. Tall and lean, the young man was dressed in tailored black slacks and a designer shirt that caressed the elegant lines of his body. A mop of artfully highlighted dark blond hair shifted as he bent to review the restaurant menu, straining the cloth of his pants against a lovely rounded bottom.

She approached, the thrum of her vampire desire riding high, and he lifted his head and swiveled it slowly in her direction. His blue-eyed gaze brightened, welcoming her.

Success, Stacia thought.

## Chapter 4

*She's here*, Alex realized, catching a glimpse of her through the crowd in the Widget.

The captivating woman from the night before.

As he moved to the edge of the dance floor, he finally had a moment to see all of her. All mouthwatering woman in a sexy red dress that displayed her lusciously curved body. A petite body, he realized as he neared.

Up until then, there had been something so larger-than-life about her that he hadn't appreciated that she barely reached midchest.

He walked the few steps until he stood before her, tilting his head down to meet her inquiring gaze. A deep, almost fathomless gaze, and this close, he confirmed his earlier suspicions that she looked totally like the demon in his dreams. That realization was so powerful that he almost reeled back as if struck, but somehow he controlled his reaction.

Her gaze narrowed and skipped across his face before the ghost of a smile came to her lips.

"Do we know each other?" she said, but a bright stain of color erupted on her face, and she shook her head and looked away.

He didn't know what to expect from his demon's doppelgänger. Certainly not such embarrassed femininity that was so at odds with the attitude he had witnessed from the vampire in his dreams and on the night he had almost died.

But then he reminded himself that one was a figment of his imagination while the woman standing before him...

The woman before him was real and sexy and not a monster.

Almost as if to verify that, he touched her,

tucking his index finger beneath her chin, but as he did so, a jolt of preternatural power surged through his body, making him pull back.

She lifted her head then. Slowly. Regally, as if his simple touch had somehow violated her rank or station in life. The earlier blush vanished and hardness crept onto her features.

"Do we know each other?" she asked once again, and this time her voice held a determined note of command.

A stain of power difficult to ignore.

"I'm not sure," he answered honestly, uncertain of whether or not meeting in his dreams would count. He was sure that she couldn't be the vampire he had met on the night he had almost died.

The answer seemed to satisfy her, since she gave a quick dip of her head. With a flick of her wrist, she sent a very obvious suggestion to her young date to disappear, which he did, scurrying away like a whipped dog.

Alex watched the young man leave and said, "Harsh."

The end Stacia had envisioned for her date

later that night was far more callous, but she contained that reply and instead said, "Would you like to dance?"

She surprised herself by asking. By the lame way she had responded to him, stammering and tossing out the most inane of questions in much the same way she had been approached hundreds of times during her long life.

And then there had been that simple touch of his hand on her chin…

His touch had reached deep into her core. As if a connection had existed between them in some other time or life. Unlikely that there was a tie, but the depth of her response was unusual.

Men rarely affected her so. Maybe "never affected her so" might have been more accurate.

Since her fateful engagement to Cassius, she had closed herself off to the wiles of men. But there was something about this man that was both familiar and demanding.

"I'd love to dance," he finally said.

Without further prompting, he took a step closer to her, began to shift to the music.

Moving his body to the pulsing beats, he teased her with an occasional brush of his body until she had to have more. She eliminated the distance between them, pressing against him. Delighting in all his hard muscle and the beat of his heart. Inhaling his enticing masculine scent.

She buried her head against the gap of skin exposed by the V of his shirt to savor that scent. Took a quick lick of his skin because she needed it, as if she'd had a bite of him in the past and been denied sustenance for too long.

As the taste of him registered, vivid images came to her of where she had seen him before, lying nearly dead in an abandoned Manhattan apartment. How they were bound to each other.

His blood.

His sweat.

The tears dashing down his face as he believed that his beloved Diana was dying. That he was dying.

Only he wasn't dead, and neither was Diana.

He had survived that fateful night in New

York. The night she had given him her vampire kiss and provided the possibility of surviving what should have been mortal wounds.

She sucked in a breath and jerked away, shocked by the insight. Losing her normally unflappable restraint over the power that allowed her thoughts, her visions, to wash over him.

He stiffened beside her as the turbulence from her mind bathed him in her memories. Shaking his head as if by doing so he could free himself of their dominion, he then relented and met her gaze.

"It wasn't just a nightmare," he said.

Stacia reined in her emotions, wrenching back the memory of that night. The taste of his blood and sweat. The too-human tears that she had thought she no longer could shed and the love for another that had been visible on his face even as he lay dying.

No, not dying, she cautioned herself and forced a wave of her vampire power to control him and curb his emotions, but surprisingly, she sensed him pushing back. Fighting her dominion.

"I want to know the truth," he said, daring to place a hand at her waist once more.

"No, you don't," she said, finding herself in a rare situation. Those conjoined memories involved caring beyond which she was capable of either understanding or giving.

"I *need* to know," he repeated, the strength of his conviction strong.

So powerful that it challenged her rule over him.

She wasn't used to being defied. Only the most powerful of vampires would dare, and those who had done so in the past had usually ended up dead, but she didn't want to waste this intriguing man.

At least, not just yet.

Leaning close, she allowed the tips of her breasts to brush against his chest and got on tiptoe until her lips were barely an inch from his.

"You want to know?" she said and released only a scintilla of her elder power, rousing desire in him in order to both punish his disobedience and entice him into cooperating.

A shudder worked across his body at her actions and awakened a sharp arousal.

His erection pressed into her belly, and he wrapped an arm around her waist, bent and whispered into her ear, "What are you doing to me?"

"You wanted to know so stop fighting this. Allow yourself to enjoy it," she said against the side of his face, slipping her hands through his short-cropped hair. Enjoying the sleekness of the strands on her fingers.

"Enjoy it? Do all your men enjoy it?" Alex cupped her buttocks and pressed her ever tighter, caught up in the spell of her power. Groaning as she moved her hips back and forth across his erection, but even as he did so, he battled the need pulling at him. Fought against her control.

It wasn't real, he told himself.

*She* wasn't real. She was a demon. A vampire. Or maybe he was crazy. Maybe he was insane, because vampires did not exist.

"This is empty. Dead," he said and yanked away from her, clearly surprising her as the power holding him in its grasp vanished like a soap bubble in the wind.

She stared at him, her face reflecting a myriad of emotions.

Bewilderment.

Anger.

Yearning.

The last startled him, but he masked his own turbulent feelings as she asked, "Who are you?"

"Alex Garcia," he said, so befuddled by her that he failed to provide the alias he used when on assignment. He cautiously held his hand out in introduction, almost afraid of touching her once again.

She glanced at his hand, seemingly as wary, then finally took hold as she replied, "Stacia."

"Stacia. No last name?"

She shook her head. "No last name."

"Like Madonna and Cher. Very eighties of you," he said, dragging up some humor in the hopes of dispelling the rather uncomfortable moment they were sharing.

She chuckled at his jest and shook her head, then glanced up at him, obviously intrigued. Just as he was fascinated on various levels: the dying agent who had imagined the demon's kiss and needed to know the truth about that night and the man who crazily found her infinitely beautiful and sexy.

"Would you like to go somewhere more quiet? Somewhere we can talk?"

A hesitant but beguiling smile came to her lips. "I'd like that very much."

## *Chapter 5*

The shop—an eclectic hole-in-the-wall offering tapas, wine, coffee and pastries—was a short walk away from Lincoln Drive on the fringe of Española Way.

They had been silent as they strolled toward the historic district. His hand rode at the small of her back. The pressure of it was light, although she felt it as strongly as if she were chained to him.

At the shop he held the door for her and she entered. With a quick greeting to the waiter, Alex ushered her toward a table for two at the back, close to a brick wall and beside the plate-glass windows that made up the exterior wall of the establishment. He offered her the seat where her back would be exposed, not that it mattered to her. With her powers she could sense danger coming.

It clearly made a difference to him, she thought, watching as he eased into the chair opposite her with the wall at his back.

"You come here often?" Before he could answer, a waiter approached and offered them menus, then left.

"I meet my clients here on occasion," he said, and was about to pick up the menu but paused and narrowed his gaze. "If I'm willing to accept that you're a vam—"

"I *am* even though I sense you still do not truly believe," Stacia replied, able to read the doubts swirling in his mind. Although she didn't know why, she wanted to shock him. Shake away the seeming calm he was exhibiting outwardly. "I eat food on occasion. People a lot more frequently."

His color paled a bit beneath the olive tones of his skin, but other than that, there was nothing to give away his reaction. "Do you mind if I choose, then? The food, that is."

Stacia chuckled, admiring his bravado. In other circumstances, she would understand that real bravery didn't rest beneath the surface, but in his case she knew differently. He was a man who didn't run from danger, which could explain his reaction to her.

"Please do while I scope out a possible dessert," she said, coquettishly glancing around the room, wishing to provoke his calm about her vampire state.

Alex had no doubt she was seriously trying to discomfit him, but he refused to buy into her game. He had already had a taste of the unusual and inexplicable power of which she seemed capable, so her actions now were more like those of a cat toying with a mouse.

He didn't much care for her games.

Still, he remained captivated while recognizing that such attraction might not necessarily be good for him. Even if he refused to believe that she was a vampire, he couldn't deny that she seemed to possess powers he could not immediately explain.

After the waiter returned to the table, Alex placed an order for some cheeses, an assortment of tapas and a bottle of red wine. The wine arrived well before the food, and after the waiter poured it, Stacia picked up her glass and offered a toast.

"To friends in common," she said, before taking a sip.

Alex swigged down a healthy amount and nodded. "I'm assuming you mean Diana and Ryder."

"I do, but Diana was more than a friend to you, wasn't she?"

Alex met her gaze full-on and answered truthfully because he sensed that she would be able discern a lie. "We were lovers back in college. And you?"

"Not lovers yet, but I keep trying," she said with a wicked grin that created havoc with his innards and had him chuckling at her cojones. He'd always had a thing for women with brass.

"So why are you here in Miami, then? Manhattan seems like a better location to accomplish that objective."

She made a moue with her mouth, swirled the wine around and averted her gaze by developing an intense interest in the fingers of ruby-red wine along the edges of the glass.

"Diana and Ryder aren't the kind for three-somes. Besides, things got...tedious in New York."

Tedious? he wondered. The last word he would use to describe anything involving Diana Reyes, his FBI agent ex-lover, was *tedious*. It made him wonder what had really driven Stacia from Manhattan. Something radical, if he accepted that she was a vampire of intense power. Not that he did.

He was about to press her on the comment, but the waiter returned with their order and placed the various tapas in the center of the table. Alex invited Stacia to sample the dishes, but she demurred.

"You first, please. It's really not what satisfies an elder like me," she admitted, even while taking another sip of the wine, which had him wondering if vampires could get drunk. Of course, that had him wondering why he was even considering such a thing as the existence of vampires.

"Was it you that night? In New York?" he asked, deciding to press for anything more concrete to substantiate her claims and sat-

isfy his own desire to find out what had really happened that night.

His hand was resting on the tabletop, and
she covered it with hers and softly said,
"What do you think?"

Before he could answer, another rush of
unnatural power swept over him, filling his
body with need and his brain with images—
vivid, almost-real memories of that night.

*Her memories.*

He sucked in a breath, battling the visions.
Sweat trickled down the back of his neck
from the effort until she whispered softly
and her words echoed in his head.

*Let me in, Alex. Don't fight it. Let me in.*

He relented. The rush of her thoughts
pummeled his mind, invading it, but her
emotions rushed in, as well.

Her rage as she entered the room and
viewed the carnage. The two dead CDA
members on the ground. He and Diana both
near death from their wounds.

She was angry because, as an immortal,
she understood the value of life, maybe more
so than those with a finite existence.

As she knelt before him, his tears yanked

pity from her. Pity at his pain as he contemplated that his ex-lover might be dying, coupled with his own regret at what might have been. At the life he would not have.

But then another sentiment overwhelmed those human emotions—the hunger to feed as she leaned close and tasted him.

Suddenly, that emotion evaporated, chased away by unexpected reactions: sorrow and need.

He sensed her despair mingled with a long-denied desire for love.

Her sharp gasp at his discovery broke the mental connection she had established.

As their gazes met, he realized that she had allowed him to see more than she had wanted to reveal. That she had exposed a piece of herself she had probably kept sheltered from others for quite a long time. Maybe she had even kept those emotions buried deep within herself because to acknowledge them was dangerous.

In her gaze he saw what she expected him to do with that revelation—that he use that vulnerability against her. Maybe even abuse that unintended admission, it occurred to him, sensing that beneath her bluster she had suffered in her life. That she wasn't as all-powerful as she wished for him to believe.

But he also sensed that, despite the hardship, she had somehow survived and possessed great mental fortitude.

Her strength proved even more enticing to him than her attractive physical shell. Because of that, he would not abuse the weakness she had exposed to him. Gently he took her hand into his and softly said, "Thank you."

"Thank you?" she repeated, clearly shocked by his actions.

"Yes, thank you. Since that night I've doubted my sanity at times. I've relived every minute through nightmares. More often than was good. And I've suffered as I wondered if I was losing my mind," he confessed, offering her his own weaknesses.

Would she abuse that disclosure or provide him yet another reason to be interested in her? he wondered.

"There are scarier things than dreams that can come to you at night," she said, withdrawing her hand from his, clearly unused to such gentleness or gratitude.

"Like you?" he challenged, arching one brow as he took another sip of his wine.

His comment dragged a devilish smile to her full lips.

"You *should* be afraid of me," she said, but it was almost as if she was trying to remind herself of what she was since whatever connection had occurred between them had somehow lessened her scariness factor.

"I'll try to remember that," he joked, earning a broadening of her smile.

She had a beautiful one, but he somehow knew it didn't come easily. It didn't fit the persona she preferred to show to the world. A persona she had likely adopted to protect herself from the earlier hurt she had inadvertently revealed to him.

But the smile fit this human persona she was showing him quite nicely.

Picking up a piece of cheese and topping it with a paper-thin slice of serrano ham, he brought it to her lips. Seemingly understanding that he wasn't going to press further about the fateful night of their first meeting, she opened her mouth and accepted his offering, but as she did so, she playfully bit his thumb and said, "Tasty."

He grinned, and when she mimicked his actions, presenting him with a bite of cheese and ham, he grasped her hand and accepted the food. Licked the tip of her index finger before sucking it into his mouth.

"Tastier," he said, playing her game.

Stacia barely controlled the shiver that worked through her body and the painful need his actions roused.

"Why are you doing this?" She was confused by what he thought he would accomplish, as well as sensing this was one human who was going to be quite difficult to control.

"Because I don't believe in monsters or things that go bump in the night."

He was testing her, not that she would be stupid enough to morph into her demon in so public a place.

"Maybe when we finish, we should go somewhere private so I can eliminate any doubts you might have."

"Maybe" was all he said as he picked

up an olive and popped it into his mouth. Followed that up with a piece of bread and cheese before he said, "What were you doing tonight at the Widget?"

"Seasoning a prospective meal," she answered honestly, needing to create distance between them because she was feeling too exposed. "What were you doing there?"

Alex sipped his wine. "Looking for a man."

"You didn't strike me as a switch-hitter." Stacia chuckled and then took an olive from the assorted tapas on the table and popped it into her mouth.

After a hearty laugh, Alex leaned closer and said, "The man might have a connection to a friend's missing daughter."

So he had been on the job, she thought, wondering what he did here in Miami. Whether it was the same kind of work that had nearly gotten him killed in New York. Realizing that discretion was necessary as long as they were in public, she also shifted closer and asked as softly as she could, "Is it part of your assignment here?"

"It's part of what I do." The silence that

followed those few words confirmed to her that there was little else he could say without compromising his position. Because she didn't want the night to end since she was enjoying his presence, she asked, "Did you grow up in Miami?"

"Born and raised, although my parents came here from Cuba."

"Ah, Cuba. It was a beautiful place the last time I visited." She didn't add that her visit had been in the 1600s, but somehow he understood not to ask.

"And you? Where were you—"

"Lived and died in Rome," she immediately answered, hardening his earlier smile into a tight, thin line.

"If I believe what all logic says, I shouldn't—"

"Believe," she urged, understanding his conflict and the angst it brought him in his nightmares. Believing was a first step to dealing with all that upset and accepting the truth about what she was.

About what had really happened that night. Maybe then he could drive those bad dreams from his mind.

"*If* I believe what you say as true, then I guess it would seem right to ask how old you were when…you know, when it happened?"

"It" being her turning, she assumed. Her death as a human and resurrection as a vampire. But it had been quite a long time since she had told that tale and she wasn't quite ready to repeat it tonight. Especially not to him. He had already touched parts of her psyche that had been closely guarded for centuries.

"That's a long story that I think would be better told at some other time."

Alex appeared to accept her reluctance and backed away. "Some other time, then," he said and motioned to the tapas remaining on the table. "Would you like a bit more? If not, I'll walk you home."

She shook her head. "That gallant gesture is wasted on me. I'm more than capable—"

"Of protecting yourself. I'm sure you are, but a gentleman always walks a lady home."

Since it seemed clear she wanted no further sustenance from the goodies he had ordered, he tossed some bills on the table and rose, offering her his arm.

To his surprise—and hers—she accepted it.

## Chapter 6

Bright and early the next morning, Alex was at his desk, perusing the inches-thick file with information the DEA had gathered over the years on the activities in the Widget.

Unfortunately, even with all their information, they had been unable to take any kind of action against the owners of the club or any of the suspects involved in the criminal activities at the location.

And what a smorgasbord of illegal activities, he thought as he flipped through the reports.

Drugs. Illegal gambling. Prostitution and

a number of missing women who had been known to frequent the Widget.

The last brought him upright in his chair. Maybe the suspects at the club were involved in more than just providing favors. Maybe they were also luring young girls into the business or even selling them, either of which could account for Andrea McAnn's alleged disappearance at the club. But of all the missing women, only Andrea had last been seen in the Widget. The others had apparently disappeared from a few of the nearby clubs.

"You seem incredibly absorbed in that file, Garcia," said Carlos Orendain, the head of his department, as he exited his office.

Orendain sauntered to Alex's workstation, thick forearms crossed against the even more muscular expanse of his chest. Since his chief barely topped five foot seven and his head seemed to rest immediately on his shoulders, all the muscle made him look like a squat fireplug.

Alex tossed the papers he had been reading onto his desk and leaned back in his chair, seemingly nonchalant. Orendain had a tendency to be controlling with his agents and their cases. He would never approve of Alex deciding to investigate the club unless it appeared as if Orendain had made the decision. With that in mind, he said, "The Widget seems like an interesting place, Chief. Lots going on there."

"Is that why you paid a visit last night?" Orendain countered.

He hid his surprise by chuckling and shaking his head. "Hell, no. I met a woman the other day and was hoping to run into her again."

And this morning he had been busy contemplating what he would do about Stacia and her claims that she was a vampire. Claims reinforced by his dreams and the scattered memories of the night he had almost died. But then again, he had been in such pain, physically and emotionally, his mind scattered from the loss of blood, that he still didn't know whether or not to believe what he thought he had seen. The fact that Stacia's claims could be true somehow didn't wipe out his fascination about her based on what little personal nuggets he had gleaned from their meeting.

Orendain plopped himself, or at least part of himself, on one corner of Alex's desk. "What did you think?"

Alex shrugged, trying to appear noncommittal. "About the woman? She was rather… unique. We spent some time—"

"Cut the bullshit. We both know you've been visiting some of our hot spots even though you were supposed to be on modified assignment."

Alex couldn't argue so he cut to the chase. "Just keeping my cover intact in case you decide to let me go back undercover, Chief."

His boss considered him through narrowed eyes, his head tilted to the side, clearly attempting to discern if the subservient pose was a ruse. When his chief's eyes widened with surprise and undisguised glee, Orendain said, "This is a change, Garcia."

Definitely, he thought. In the past they had always been at odds because of Orendain's nature and his own. Their last big battle had been about Alex's agreeing to the undercover assignment up in New York. His boss had warned him about the mission, and in a way, Orendain had been right.

The assignment had chewed him up and spit him up into pieces he was still trying to put back together.

"I learned a thing or two in New York," Alex admitted with another nonchalant shrug as he looked down at the papers on his desk.

A bigger man might have held back, but Orendain was big only in terms of muscle. "Hate to say I told you so, but—"

"You were right that the assignment would show me what I was made of," he said, not that his chief would take that statement in a positive light. He kept to himself that the mission had also proved to him that he was a man who held others above himself. A man who accepted the pain of losing someone he loved. Twice, because he knew that someone else could make her happier.

"Damn straight," his boss replied with some relish and jerked his finger in the direction of the reports on the club. "I know the doctors cleared you for duty, but are you ready for an undercover assignment?"

Alex nodded, picked up the papers on his desk and held them up in the air. "There's a lot going on at this club. It would be quite a coup for you if we found a way to shut it down or brought in some of the bigger dealers."

"You finally understand, Garcia," Orendain said with a smug smile. "See what else you can find out. See if we have enough for you to investigate it further," his boss added, rising from his desk and swaggering away.

As he watched him go, Alex thought, *I do understand.* If finding Dan's daughter meant sucking up to Orendain, he was willing to go along with it.

Others above self, he thought, opening the file and turning toward his computer. If he was going to convince Orendain that he should investigate what was happening at the club, he would need a lot more than Dan's missing daughter to do it.

Stacia roused in the late afternoon with an odd sense of lethargy.

She wrote it off to being unable to feed last night thanks to her meeting with Alex Garcia.

Alex had certainly been looking far better than he had the first time she had run into him. Then again, he had been on death's door, bleeding from a couple of gunshot wounds and barely conscious.

She was surprised that he had remembered seeing her.

She had assumed that he had been too far gone to recall their encounter, but he had apparently remembered quite a bit about that meeting. And he had clearly seen her demon face. But from their talk last night, it was obvious that he still doubted his recollections even though she had made no bones about confirming his suspicions.

Of course, seeing was believing, only…

His audacity was enticing. It had been some time since anyone had actually dared to fight back against her power. And his attraction to her was unmistakable, despite his trying to deny it.

Real human attraction, she acknowledged, untainted by the thrall of vampire power.

For the first time in a long time, she could see a temporary respite from her ennui by spending some time with the good-looking law-enforcement officer. She could even picture herself sharing a pleasant interlude with

Alex. After all, he was quite handsome in that Latin kind of way with his dark hair, olive skin and amazingly green eyes.

As for his body...

They hadn't had much of a chance to dance last night, but she suspected he would be able to easily handle carrying her with those broad shoulders. Build her passion with those mobile hips and bring her pleasure with that engaging mouth while that intense gaze absorbed every last little detail.

But just to make sure she was not wrong about all that he could provide...

She had decided to put Alex to the test tonight. Push him to the limit and see how he would respond. She had no hesitation as to where to find him—she was certain he would be back in the club tonight. He had said as much last night when he had dropped her off at her door, ever the gentleman until she had grabbed hold of his shirt and hauled him close for a hard, demanding kiss. They had both been shaking by the time he had pulled away, and for a moment, she had considered using her elder power to bring him under control, but only for a moment. For the first time in centuries, she wanted to explore the attraction between them, free and clear of the vampire's stain.

First, however, she had to feed. But the blood-bank bags she had in the minifridge would do little to satisfy the hunger she had worked up by skipping last night's meal.

With the worst of the afternoon sun gone, she could venture outside where there would be dozens of humans walking around. A forceful mental suggestion and a darkened corner somewhere would provide her the vamp equivalent of fast food.

Needing that sustenance, she dressed as if for a jog and made her way to the lobby. One attractive young woman, similarly dressed, was exiting the hotel via a side door.

Stacia recalled that there was a small building that housed a gym at the back of the hotel grounds. Following the female, she confirmed that the runner was going to the gym.

Stacia followed.

The young woman entered the building with Stacia just a few steps behind her. The gym was empty of people. Only a few pieces of equipment and a television were in the room. Immediately the woman took a spot on the treadmill, but before she could push a button, Stacia was sending the runner a message.

*Come with me,* Stacia commanded and held out her hand.

The woman had little willpower. She faced Stacia like a lamb to slaughter and then stepped off the treadmill. She wasn't as young as she first appeared, Stacia realized now that the woman was closer. In her mid-thirties if Stacia had to guess, not that she was all that good at estimating mortal ages. After nearly two thousand years of immortal life, humans in the twenty-to-forty category all seemed to blur together.

But the woman was fit and fairly attractive.

Her body had the long lean, lines of a runner, with B-cup breasts that were so far defying gravity beneath the confines of the sports bra she wore.

*Come,* Stacia urged again and increased the force of her elder power until a semi-glazed look slipped onto the woman's face.

"That's it," Stacia nearly purred, and the woman eased her hand into Stacia's.

With a gentle tug, Stacia urged her toward the back of the gym and away from the glass doors facing the hotel's gardens. There was an odd jag in the wall there, hiding the entrance to a supply room. Stacia urged the woman into that hidey-hole and pressed her against the door of the supply room. Raising her hand, she caressed the smooth line of the woman's jaw.

"Who are you?" the woman managed to ask despite Stacia's control.

Stacia leaned close, brushed a kiss across the women's lips and said, "Someone who can give you great pleasure."

With those words, she unleashed even more of her elder power and the woman gasped, her body caught up in the ardor that Stacia called forth in her. As Stacia examined the woman's body, she saw that her nipples had gone hard and the aroma of the arousal brought on by the surge of vampire rule perfumed the air.

"Enjoy," she said, cupping the woman's

chin with her thumb and forefinger to expose her neck.

"Touch yourself," Stacia whispered against the shell of her captive's ear and the woman complied, reaching up to caress her own breasts.

Poor thing might as well get some enjoyment from this, Stacia thought. Besides, a little sexual stimulation always gave the blood a nice flavor, she thought as she inched up on tiptoe and allowed the demon to emerge.

A tremor of need slinked across Stacia's body as her fangs burst forth and the world around her exploded into almost painful brilliance.

Everything became more vivid. More demanding, almost a violent assault on Stacia's senses.

The woman's soft moan as she played with herself was loud in Stacia's ears, but not nearly loud enough to drown out the rushed *lub-dub lub-dub* as the runner's heartbeat accelerated from her growing pleasure.

As Stacia met the woman's glazed eyes, her own gaze now the demon's startling blue-green, a scared little mewl burst from the woman's lips, but Stacia stroked the side of the runner's neck lovingly, attempting to temper the fear.

"Do not worry, love. You will enjoy this," Stacia urged, rising on tiptoe and brushing the razor-fine tips of her fangs across the delicate softness of the woman's skin.

The woman surprised her then, reaching up to cup the back of Stacia's head. The racing of her heartbeat growing faster while the intoxicating smell of her pleasure/fear wrapped around Stacia's senses.

It was difficult to contain her own little moan of anticipation. She allowed herself that release only a second before she closed her eyes and sank her fangs deep into the woman's neck.

The runner's blood was rich, filled with healthy, vital human. Flavored with the woman's desire, which sizzled through Stacia's veins, awakening every cell. Yanking forth need in her vampire body. Demanding satisfaction.

*Touch me,* she mentally commanded the woman even as she continued draining her of her life's blood. *Touch me now,* she telepathed more urgently and the woman finally complied, cradling Stacia's breast. Finding the sensitized tip beneath the fabric of Stacia's shirt.

Stacia moaned, gave a deeper, harder pull against the woman's neck as she became lost in the needs of the demon.

Blood and sex.

Sex and blood.

Her heart raced to the beats of their call. Her body pulsed with the satisfaction of the feeding and the sex, but then Alex's face replaced that of the woman and his words came to her.

Condemning. Almost deafening.

*This is so empty. Dead.*

The words ricocheted through her brain, along with the image of his compelling gaze sweeping over her. Calling to the woman and not the demon.

With a strangled moan of frustration, Stacia ripped away from the runner, all pleasure gone, twisted need sated for the moment.

The woman protested Stacia's abandonment, still caught up in the thrum of Stacia's elder power and the sexual awakening of the demon. But she had been weakened by the feeding and slowly crumpled back against the supply-room door and then down to the floor, her gaze locked on Stacia the entire time.

Accusing.

Grateful.

Even now, with the twin marks of Stacia's fangs slowly closing along her neck, the woman was still in the throes of desire, her eyes dilated and the tips of her breasts rock hard. Her hands caressed those tips, working them for a moment until Stacia totally withdrew her control over the woman and the blood loss finally pulled the runner into unconsciousness.

Stacia whirled and fled the gym, unnoticed.

The woman within the gym would recover.

Stacia hadn't taken enough blood to cause permanent injury. And her vampire's kiss would keep the woman from remembering, although the thrall of demon desire might linger for a bit longer.

The woman's partner, if she had one,

might thank her for that, she thought, but Alex's words came again, mocking her.

*Dead.*

*Empty.*

Damn him, she thought. Damn him for making her want more. Damn him for remembering the kiss she had given him that night. It was rare for mortals to remember, but so far Alex had proved that he was not just another human. Or maybe it was due to how close to death he had been when she had kissed him. After all, she remembered that moment that Cassius had stolen her life. Made her as dead as Alex claimed.

Damn him, she thought again. Tonight she would find Alex and prove to him just how alive and fulfilling she could be.

## Chapter 7

Alex sat across from one of his contacts at Vida Loca, another of the clubs that some of the missing women had visited. This establishment was about half the size of the Widget, but with a totally different vibe. It was done up with a theme that was part jungle, part urban in keeping with the music the bar usually offered, a mix of hip-hop, Latin and reggaeton.

The walls had been rough plastered and covered with graffiti. Jungle vines, tropical flora and fauna had then been painted over the graffiti as if the jungle had taken over the city. In the outdoor courtyard behind the building, the mix of styles continued, but the walls bore live bougainvillea and an assortment of other tropical plants.

The club was not nearly as crowded as the Widget. The crowd tonight appeared to be a mix of thirtysomethings and European tourists. Because of that, there was a mellow mood in the air. In response to the nature of the crowd, the DJ was spinning a mix of slow tunes and Top 40s, which allowed the patrons to sit and chat and nosh on the limited food options offered on the menu.

The mood was perfect for the meeting he had scheduled with an informant who had provided information on the Sheik and another drug dealer—Carlos Delgado. His informant had news on them and their involvement in the beating of one of the missing women's boyfriends. The boyfriend had decided to play detective and paid a huge price for it. He was currently in a local hospital in a coma.

"If I told you I wanted to find some company—" Alex began, but his contact, Luis

Alvarado—Louie to his friends—immediately cut him off.

"Male or female?"

Alex arched an eyebrow. "What do you think?"

"Female, but it never hurts to ask, Alejandro. The answer sometimes surprises you," Louie said. "For the night or for something more permanent?"

"More permanent?" Alex repeated. "Do I strike you as the marrying type?" he added in jest.

Louie shook his head and chuckled. "Again, makes sense to ask. So do you want a by-the-hour girl or..."

"Or what?" Alex picked up his drink, seltzer with mint and a twist of lime to fool people into thinking he was downing mojitos.

Louie leaned closer and looked around, clearly uneasy. Seemingly satisfied that it was safe to continue after his perusal of the patrons in the club, he said, "Rumor has it that arrangements can be made to provide you with someone you can keep for a while."

"A while as in—"

"Until you get tired of her. Then you can

trade her in," Louie said and picked up a glass with a shot of whiskey straight up.

"Trade her in? Like for a newer model?" Alex said, but as he did so, he caught sight of Stacia walking into the club. She looked as amazing as she had the night before, only this time she was wearing a formfitting dress in a shade of blue like the sunlit Caribbean. Her hips rolled from one side to the next, pulling his interest to that enticing movement.

"Filipino. Korean. You name it," Louie said, his gaze narrowing as he realized Alex had become distracted.

"American. What if I wanted a nice all-American girl," Alex jumped in, keeping half his attention on Louie and the other on Stacia as she sashayed to the bar.

"*¿Americana? ¿Estas loco?*" Louie warned and turned in his chair to track Alex's gaze and find out the source of his inattention. He immediately caught sight of Stacia. "*Dios mío,* but that is one fine piece of ass."

Louie went to rise, but Alex snared his arm and forced him back down. "That woman is off-limits, Louie. So what about a nice *Americana?*"

"I get it. Interested in a little threesome," the other man said with a chuckle and turned to leer at Stacia. "The *Americanas* go overseas, *amigo.* Too many complications in keeping them here. Plus, I hear Delgado's getting lots of blow in exchange for the *Americanas.*"

"You mentioned Delgado was into big enough quantities to become a supplier to various dealers. He's getting the blow in exchange for the women?" Alex asked, wanting to make sure he understood what Louie meant. Feeling dirty and disgusted by the whole concept of trading drugs for women.

"Quite a few kilos for one *Americana.* At least that's what I'm hearing. It's why Delgado's no longer selling on the street. He's moving on up." Louie picked up his drink and slugged it down. Slammed the empty glass on the table and asked, "So are you interested? I can find out where the action is going down. For the right price, that is."

Alex reached into his pocket and withdrew two hundred-dollar bills, his usual payment for the information Louie provided. "I'd like to meet Delgado's suppliers. Tell them I can pay in cash for the blow. Lessen their risk in dealing women. Maybe even make an investment in their operation if the stuff they're bringing in is quality."

Louie nodded and covered the bills on the table. Palmed them so as to not make the exchange so obvious. "What else is in it for me if I can make the arrangement?"

"More of what you just got. Lots more," Alex said, thinking that he could arrange for a larger payment from DEA informant funds if Louie could come through for him.

"I'll see what I can find out," Louie said.

Alex nodded and rose without waiting for his informant as he spotted a young man moving into the space beside Stacia at the bar.

He headed over, telling himself it was to spare the man from becoming her next meal, but he was lying to himself. First because he wasn't quite sure he was buying into the whole vampire thing. Growing up in Miami surrounded by Santeria, voodoo and an assortment of other beliefs, he'd seen what could be done with psychic abilities. That could explain that rush of energy she had cast over him and the way she had shared her memories with him. He remembered one time that his grandmother had invited over a *santero* when his granddad had passed. After the *santero* and his grandmother had paid homage to the statue of Santa Barbara on the small table in his home, there had been a change in the air around them. The *santero* had touched his grandmother's face then, and the look in her eyes had been so compelling, Alex had wandered closer. The *santero* had brushed a hand across his hair, much as his grandfather had done all his life. He had felt his grandfather then, as if he had been standing right beside him.

Maybe Stacia had similar powers.

But secondly, and if he were being totally honest, he had to stop denying that he wanted her all to himself, because he found her to be a fascinating mix of strength and vulnerability.

As he approached, she swiveled on her bar stool and her lips slowly tilted upward. It was a calculating smile, as if she had been well aware all along that he was in the club and would eventually come her way. As she had done the night before, she flicked her hand, her long, graceful fingers elegantly waving through the air dismissively.

The young man who had been beside her rose and scurried away.

A bit of misplaced male pride that he was her choice added a slight swagger to his walk. When he neared, he bent close and whispered against the shell of her ear, "*Querida.* I didn't expect to see you again so soon."

"*Mentiroso,*" she teased, calling him a liar and surprising him with her knowledge of Spanish. She ran her hand down the front of his shirt, the touch of her fingers flirtatiously light. His shirt was open to midchest, and as her hand trailed down and then up, the tip of her index finger slipped beneath the fabric and against his skin, sending a tendril of desire snaking through his body.

Taking up her challenge, he faced her, his lips barely an inch away from hers. Confessing his interest, he said, "I'd only be a liar if I said I wasn't glad to see you."

His breath spilled against Stacia's face,

warm with life. He smelled of lime and mint, and the wicked grin on his face was alive with defiance once more, as were his words.

He tucked his thumb and forefinger beneath her chin and tilted her face upward. Before it could register in her mind what he intended, his lips were on hers. Soft. Mobile. Opening and closing against her mouth enticingly. Dragging her eyes shut as she battled the sensation and taste of being kissed.

And kissed amazingly well.

Her mind whirled with the headiness of it. Of his mouth inviting her to open to his. His tongue lightly danced along the edge of her lips, both daring and hesitant.

She had been waiting for another kiss like this since last night, Stacia thought, laying her hand on his shoulder to steady herself as she answered his demand, opening her mouth to accept the sweet slide of his tongue. Nipping at it with her teeth—human teeth—and at the edges of his lips, so full, so heated, so human.

Human, she reminded herself as a curl of heat ignited deep within her and slowly spread throughout her body, awakening the demon.

She battled back the vampire, wanting to bask in the delight of his attention. Savoring his honest but conflicted passion.

She could sense that in him, the struggle. Mirroring her own disturbance at the desire he had awakened.

The tendrils of that turmoil curled around their hearts and into the kiss, slowly strangling the need. Pulling them apart as they tempered what remained of their passion.

His hand trembled against the side of her face as he cradled it and ran his thumb across her lips, clearly reluctant. His gaze focused on her lips until he slowly lifted it upward and a puzzled look swept across his features.

"Your eyes. They're blue now," he said, raising his hand to brush a finger along the line of her brow.

The demon's eyes, she thought, surprised she had not been able to contain that aspect of the vampire. She was an elder, after all, and should have been totally in control. Reining in that bit of herself, the even more confused look on his face confirmed that the normal brown of her eyes had returned.

"What was that?" He dropped onto the bar stool beside her.

She picked up her drink, surprised to see a slight quaver in her hand, and took a bracing sip of the wine. The bold body of it washed away the taste of him, all citrus and mint.

So Miami.

"Do you really want to know?" she asked, staring straight ahead to avoid engaging him. Afraid of what she might see in his eyes if she dared to look at him.

Alex considered her evasion and her question. He realized that he might not want to know.

At least, not yet.

His body was heavy with the need created by their kiss. A kiss that had started out simply and yet had built into something so much more exciting. He could still taste her—willing woman and wine. He licked his lips, wishing he could relish her again, but she had withdrawn from him.

Had he scared her away?

But if she was some big-shot vampire as

she claimed, how could a mortal man have her running?

Not that he was buying into the whole vampire thing. That was still too outrageous for him to consider.

*But how do you explain the eyes?* the voice in his head taunted, but he drove it away, too intrigued by all the other aspects of the woman sitting beside him.

"Are you free?" he said at the same time that she asked, "Are you busy?"

The moment eased a bit of the tension as they both chuckled and shook their heads. When they shot glances at each other, their gazes were tentative and yet captivated.

Alex shifted to the edge of the stool, drawing close to her once again so he could whisper, "I need to stay here for a little while, then make a call. Maybe check out the Widget."

At the mention of the latter, she crinkled up the straight line of her nose and swirled the wine in her glass.

"I don't care for that club myself—" he began.

"But you've got a job to do," she finished.

"I won't be long. How about I get you a fresh glass of wine and we take a seat near the back?" he offered, motioning for the waiter even before she had answered.

"Sure of yourself, aren't you?" she said, but didn't argue with him when he grabbed the two glasses of wine the bartender put on the table and told the man to add the drinks to his tab.

He invited her to walk before him and Stacia did, adding an enticing sway to her hips in an effort to topple his seeming control and confidence. It had been too long since a man had had that kind of power over her, and the last time it had happened, it hadn't ended well for her.

She was not about to be bested again. Her heart had been safe for too long and she was not about to risk it again, especially not for a mere mortal.

No matter how interesting he might be, she admitted.

## Chapter 8

Toward the back of the club, a table for two was open and she sat down, waiting for him to join her. As with the seating from the night before, the wall was to his back, the entire club visible from the spot she had chosen.

"Still looking for a man?" she asked when he took a place beside her.

He scooted his chair close and wrapped his arm around her shoulders. His fingers brushed along the bare skin exposed by her strapless dress. With a wry grin, he whispered against the side of her face, "Two, actually."

"A ménage," she teased and faced him, her nose brushing the rasp of evening beard along the defined line of his jaw. The innocent action made her think about having him trail that sandpapery skin across assorted parts of her body. It brought a blush to her cheeks, and although he noticed it, he didn't seize on it as she expected.

He was proving to be far less predictable than other mortals she had encountered over her long existence. That unpredictability was turning out to be quite an aphrodisiac, along with his compassion and honor.

"You might say that. Rumor has it they're into all kinds of nasty things." He picked up his glass and, with a quick tilt in her direction to mimic a toast, took a sip.

*Nasty things* could have so many meanings, especially for someone as old as she was. In her millennia of existence, she had seen nastiness he probably couldn't begin to imagine.

"Terrorist kinds of things?" she asked, recalling the nature of his assignment when he had nearly been killed in New York City.

He shook his head. "That was a onetime

gig for me. Right now I'm trying to find a friend's daughter and some other missing women." The tone of his voice was low so that she would be the only one to hear.

"Missing? Do you think they're dead?" she wondered aloud. She had sensed a number of vampires in the clubs so far, but hundreds of years ago vampire councils everywhere had come down hard on those who killed humans. It brought too much attention to their kind, and the fear provoked by such deaths often had dire consequences for the local vampire underworlds. She had barely survived genocide in Rome when panic had roused the mortals into a killing frenzy.

Meeting his gaze, she noted the concern there for the women who had gone missing. While she knew little about him, she suspected he wouldn't rest until he had an answer about their whereabouts. She also considered that none of her kind had anything to do with their disappearances. Even though there was always the possibility of a rogue vampire who would violate the elders' edicts, Alex seemed to think these disappearances were the result of mortal activities, and she wasn't about to contradict that. But she did want to know more.

"Well? Are they dead?" she prompted again at his delay.

Alex glanced around, leaned near once more and finally said, "I think there may be a white-slavery ring in operation at the Widget."

Slavery. An ugly word for an ugly practice. One from which she had suffered personally. The memories wrenched a very visceral reaction from her, which she was unable to keep in check.

The demon surged forward, its gaze becoming a phosphorescent blue-green. Fangs bursting from her mouth to extend below her upper lip before she tamed the monster and retracted her canines.

*"Dios mío,"* Alex muttered, recoiling for a moment before reaching up to cradle her cheek and run his finger along the now straight line of her teeth. Trying to convince himself that he hadn't seen a pair of fangs just seconds earlier.

"God?" she challenged, tugging his hand away from her face. "If there was a God, don't you think he would put a stop to things like slavery? To demons like me?"

Alex watched as the blue-green light bled into her eyes once again from the very evident emotions churning through her. Her hand rested on the tabletop, shifting nervously against its surface.

The gesture so telling. So human.

Only she wasn't human, he now knew. He could no longer deny what she was. No longer refute what had happened that night in Manhattan. What he had seen just moments earlier.

She was a demon.

A vampire. Undead. Immortal. A bloodsucker. A monster, except...

It was very hard to think of her that way while pain lingered in those changeling eyes. While the woman and not the demon sat beside him, uneasy. Much as he had guessed the night before, she had suffered in an earlier life.

That suffering continued to make her vulnerable and more decidedly human than some of the mortals he had met in his life.

It was what prompted an unexpected reaction from him, because in his heart he knew she needed compassion more than anything else.

He tenderly covered her hand and stilled the anxious motion. Slowly the tension left her body thanks to his comforting touch. With that release, the blue-green gaze receded and he gently curled his hand around hers, offering solace.

The questioning look on her face confirmed she was unused to such kindness.

"I can't change what happened in your life—"

"You can't even begin to imagine what's happened in my life," she shot back, the anger in her words subdued as she kept her hand in his, offering him hope that he had reached her.

"Try me."

There was a moment's hesitation before she did as he asked, twining her fingers with his. Broadcasting her memories with a long, hesitant leaking of elder power, almost as if she was afraid to trust him with those recollections.

"Trust me," he urged, tightening his grasp on her hand.

She finally released her tenuous hold and allowed him to see her past.

*Rome, nearly 2,000 years earlier*

The conflicting aromas of lavender and orange blossoms were heavy, rising along with the steam from the baths. The scents were almost overpowering as Stacia followed her beloved husband-to-be deeper into the building until he finally stopped before the biggest of the baths.

At the edge of the tiled pool sat thick towels and robes, along with a large brass tray holding a decanter, glasses and a plate with an assortment of cheeses.

"You were quite sure of yourself," she said as she noted the care with which the bath had been prepared.

"Sure of us," Cassius replied and led her to the edge of the pool, where he stood behind her. Reaching up, he slipped his hands beneath the straps of the tunic she wore. His skin was cold against hers, dragging a shiver from her.

"Nervous?" he asked, his breath skimming along the side of her face as he eased the straps from her shoulders.

Stacia flattened the fine linen of her tunic to her body as gravity pulled it downward.

"Do not fear, my wife," Cassius urged, bringing his arms around her and laying his hands over hers. He bent his head, dropped a line of kisses along the top of her shoulder and gently tugged her hands downward to reveal her breasts. Before she could protest, he covered them with his hands, tenderly kneading and massaging. He moved his mouth to the gap between her neck and shoulder, gave a quick love bite before he sucked on the sensitized spot.

"Cassius," she said softly, slipping her hand behind her to pass it over the swell of his erection as it pressed into the small of her back.

"Ah, love. You'll unman me," he whispered only a moment before he swept one hand down and undid the tie at her waist.

Her linen tunic dropped to the tiled floor, and with soft pressure on her shoulders, Cassius turned her around.

Stacia shyly covered her breasts, unused to such intimacies. Virginity was highly prized amongst Roman brides and she had been guarding that gift until their wedding night. But Cassius placed his hands over hers and tenderly urged her hands away.

"Beautiful," he said, cradling a breast in each hand and strumming his thumbs along the dark caramel tips of her breasts. The action created a throbbing deep between her legs, and as he tightened his hold, tweaking the tips, she released a surprised gasp at the sensations rocketing through her body.

"I can smell your need," her beloved said, a strange purr entering his voice. He raised one hand and cradled the back of her head, forcing her gaze up to meet his.

She saw it then, a growing glitter of blue-green bleeding into the almost black of his irises.

"Cassius?" she questioned, sensing a shimmer of something odd beside her.

He moved quickly then, wrapping an arm around her waist and spearing his fingers into her hair, roughly imprisoning her against him, all of his earlier gentleness disappearing.

The deep brown of his gaze was now gone, totally obliterated by the odd blue-green light, and a second later she noted the first hint of white slipping past his upper lip. Alarm filled her as long, sharp fangs became lethally apparent.

The connection between them abruptly evaporated.

Alex shook his head to clear the slight daze created by the absence of it and then met Stacia's shimmering gaze.

"What happened then, Stacia? What did he do?" he asked, needing to know. Wanting to understand what had transpired in her life. How she had become what she was.

"He took my virginity and then he gave me a choice," she replied, her tone wooden, belying the obvious tumult of her emotions.

Alex arched a brow. "A choice?"

"Die or become like him," she replied, her voice flat while her eyes were alive with her distress.

He needed nothing else to guess what her choice had been and yet he wished to know more. Wanted to understand about what had made her the way she was emotionally and not just physically.

"How old were you?"

With her free hand, she picked up her wineglass. There was a telling quaver there before she took a sip of the wine and then said, "Seventeen. I was only seventeen."

Seventeen, he thought. So young to have your hopes and dreams shattered. To learn that those you loved could not be trusted.

Her eyes spoke volumes about that betrayal, which was still alive after so long.

He leaned forward and examined her more closely, looking for other signs of what she was feeling, but she had shuttered her emotions as a safeguard. As he continued to study her, he thought that she looked older than seventeen now, but not beyond her late twenties, prompting a query.

"Do vampires grow older?"

Stacia nodded and took another sip of her wine. "Very slowly. It's taken me nearly two thousand years to reach this human age, whatever it may be."

"You've aged well," he said, attempting to lighten her mood. Understanding that he had forced her to reveal a very painful history and that it was something she rarely did.

That maybe she had never revealed that past to anyone else.

His cop's gut told him that there was even more to her story that she had not laid bare. He wondered whether to press, but then considered he had offered nothing of himself during the entire exchange.

Maybe for good reason.

As he had realized earlier, he could no longer deny what she was. Could no longer reject the reality of what he had seen that fateful night in New York City. But faced with that reality and his reaction to it, he had to curb his attraction to her and not just because she was a vampire.

Alex was wise enough to understand that he had built his own defense mechanisms when Diana had pushed him out of her life and then walked away. Not once but twice.

He had relegated all his energy to his job. Avoided any complications with women to avoid the pain that came with commitment. To avoid any distractions to his career, which he had made first and foremost.

He had thought at first that Stacia might provide a pleasant break from those duties. But with all that he had discovered about her, he now understood that she was more than just a passing affair. If he truly allowed himself to explore this complex woman, she would present a dangerous distraction to the assignment he had just undertaken.

He could not afford to have anything in his life that diverted his attention from the task at hand. Not only did his life depend on it, but the lives of the women who were still missing, including Dan's daughter, hung in the balance.

Recognizing the perils he faced, he also was conscious of the fact that he had to tread carefully, but not because he feared Stacia the vampire elder.

He had to act with caution because he was beginning to care for the woman she had revealed to him.

A strong woman who had survived great hardship.

A woman who was capable of passion but seemed not to understand anything about love. Not that he was any better in that department.

"I want to thank you for sharing that," he said, and as he did so, she eased her hand from his. A sad smile came to her face.

"I understand, Alex. You don't live as long as I have and not know when a man isn't interested."

"It's not like that, Stacia. Believe me," he urged, needing for her to understand that…

What did he want her to comprehend?

He didn't know if he quite grasped the maelstrom of emotions she invoked in him or that lived beneath her seemingly calm exterior.

Stacia leaned forward, her voice heavy with despair. "In my long life I've believed in only one man, Alex. He took my innocence. Then he took my life and made me his slave."

"Not all men are like him," he urged, reaching for her again. Wishing to bring peace to her troubled spirit.

"I suppose you think you're different? That you wouldn't try to control me? Own me?" she challenged, enmity rising up once more.

He thought about his past relationships—
few and far between. Thought about the love
he had shared with Diana, probably the one
and only woman who had captured his heart.
In all the time they had been together, he had
never tried to control her.

"Never. I would never try to control you,"
he blurted out, surprised by his declaration,
because it almost hinted that there existed a
possibility for more between them.

"Never?" she repeated. She rose from the
table, her head at a regal angle. A determined
gleam in her deep brown gaze.

"I guess we'll just have to see about that
promise," she added and walked away, leaving him to appreciate the sexy roll of her
womanly hips and the tempting curves of
her petite body.

The need he had banked after their kiss
reared up again. It took all his willpower and
a few bracing gulps of the wine for him to
tamp it down and focus his attention on the
occupants of the bar.

He reminded himself that his primary
focus should be on his investigation. That
his assignment—and not Stacia—was the

reason he was here. According to Louie, both Delgado and Santos often dropped by the bar and spent time at the club.

With any luck, this place would provide him with another piece of the puzzle that he needed to find the missing women.

As for Stacia…

Whatever had been developing between them would have to wait. Although he sensed her want for more than her current state, there were other women who had a great deal more at stake.

Who needed him more than Stacia.

Because of that, he drove her from his mind and delved into gathering the information he needed for his assignment.

Andrea McAnn huddled in the corner, waiting for the moment the door to the tiny room would open. It did so once a day when it was time for the one and only feeding she would get. It had been that way since she had awoken in the nasty little room. By her count she had been there close to a week, although with no windows and barely any communication with anyone, it was tough to keep track of time.

The room was musty as was common in many of the older buildings in South Beach. Not much bigger than a closet with cinder-block walls that looked relatively new, as if they had been built recently. For the first day or so she had tried screaming for help, but the only thing it had accomplished was a sore throat. Although she thought she had heard other cries while she did so. Maybe other women, but whatever noises she had thought she had heard had stopped during the past few days.

She wondered if the other women were now gone. How they had ended up in the other rooms. How she had been taken.

The last thing she remembered was going into one of the private rooms with the Sheik. He had gotten his nickname because he had a swarthy, foreign look about him, had always been elegantly dressed and flashing lots of cash. She had been excited when he had approached her and asked her to dance. Even more intrigued when he had requested her company to go play in one of the luxurious private gaming rooms for which the club had earned a reputation.

Usually only the most elite guests went into those private areas. She and her friends had seen an assortment of celebrities enter and now she was being asked to join him there.

Omar, the Sheik's real name, had taken her into one of the lavish rooms where a state-of-the-art gaming system had been connected to an immense wall-size television. Rich rugs and pillows were strewn about the area, making her feel as if she had entered a lush harem.

Omar had offered her luscious appetizers and champagne.

As excited as she had been about being there with him, she had demurred on the champagne, recalling her promise to her father. For over a year the two of them had been sober. Andrea had wanted to stick to her promise, no matter how difficult; life had been better since making that vow.

Omar had seemed annoyed with that, but had immediately called in a waiter to bring her something else to drink.

Then they had plopped down onto the sumptuous pillows and begun to play the video game. When the soda had arrived, she had taken a sip or two and had immediately started getting dizzy.

That was the last thing she remembered.

Sitting there now, tucked into the corner with her knees drawn up tight to her chest and her arms wrapped around them, it occurred to her that the soda had been drugged. That Omar's annoyance when she refused to drink the champagne had been because it, too, had been spiked with something.

And so she went from wondering how she had been taken to why? Why would someone want to grab her? What could they possibly want? It wasn't as if she was one of the celebrities and rife with cash to pay a ransom demand. She was just an ordinary, average American girl.

She took comfort from the fact that she was being fed and offered a place to relieve herself in the far corner of the room.

If they had planned on killing her, she would be dead already, she surmised.

Which meant they wanted her alive for some reason.

She told herself not to lose hope. Her father would look for her. Either he would find her or get one of his old buddies to help discover where she was. Her dad would find her one way or another, she repeated and started to rock back and forth as she waited for the door to open once again. That small bit of food and interaction with another human gave her solace.

As long as the door opened, bringing her a meal, there was hope.

## Chapter 9

Alex's words remained with her long after Stacia left the club and made her way to another establishment and then another until she finally found herself back at the Widget, much as she despised the noise there.

*A white-slavery ring.*

Even now the words created a whirl of emotions within her.

Cassius, she thought, thinking that his name had suited him well. The name meant "an empty face," and that had sadly matched his empty heart. The heart that had betrayed her, taking first her virginity and then her life before finally stealing her freedom.

For nearly a year after siring, her he had kept her a virtual slave in their new home, away from family and friends. He had made her beholden to him for the blood needed to sustain the fragile existence of a newly made vampire. In exchange for the sustenance, Cassius had used her to satisfy whatever depraved need came to mind.

There had been many of those demands, some so vile that she still remembered them, tasted her humiliation after nearly two millennia.

Someone more fragile might not have survived the ordeal.

But she had persevered and become stronger for it, Stacia thought, examining those in the club and wondering if Alex was right about what might be happening here. Observing the men to see if she noticed anything unusual.

While she was at it, she considered the women the way an ancient Roman slave trader might have. Height. Weight. Beauty. Age.

Stacia appreciated that in this glittering

city of glamorous and dazzling people, the Roman slave trader would have had a field day.

An assortment of stunning young men and women out to enjoy a night on the town were on glittering display. Totally unaware of the danger they were in from the possible kidnappers and from demons like her.

Battling the assault of the noise on her vampire senses, she sat at the bar. Before she could place an order, a man snagged the open seat beside her and asked, "Can I get you something?"

Eyeing him up and down, it occurred to her that he was a passable companion. Not as well built or as handsome as Alex, but he would do to satisfy her needs.

"A mojito would be nice," she said, requiring something stronger than the wine she'd had earlier. Something to dull the ache of the emotions she had revealed and which still lingered. Although the alcohol did nothing to her system, memories remained of its powers and brought a sympathetic mental response.

The man motioned to the bartender, making a V with two fingers as he said, *"Dos mojitos."*

After the bartender walked away, the man grinned and held out his hand, "I'm Raul."

She shook his hand, inclined her head and, with a polite nod, provided her name.

"Stacia," Raul repeated. "A beautiful name for a beautiful woman."

She forced a smile to her lips because it was expected, while all she could think was *Lame, lame, lame* as he continued with the conversation. She answered every trite question he posed because she was feeling too lazy to go in search of anything better.

After they had finished the drink and had another, he asked her to dance. She went, eager to move the night along and take good ol' Raul someplace where she could sink her teeth into him and get her sustenance.

Much like at the club where she had met Alex earlier, the music was mellower at the Widget tonight, although still too loud for her sensitive hearing. Similarly, there was less of a crowd, allowing them more room to dance, not that her dinner seemed to notice the available space.

Within a second of hitting the floor, he pulled her near for the slow dance, leaving barely an inch of distance between them as they did an unimaginative shuffle, swaying back and forth to the slow tempo of the song.

One, two, one, two, she thought, counting down every monotonous beat. Her count was thrown off by the escalating *lub-dub* of his heartbeat as he closed the distance between them and his passion rose.

She switched her countdown to the beat of his heart, aware that with each hurried cadence her meal would soon be ready.

Stacia was so engrossed in that beat, it took her a moment to register that her date— if you could call him that—had moved away from her. But after that split second of inattention, Alex's presence registered. The smell of him and heat of his body, pulsating against vamp radar, which had been surprisingly slow in warning about his approach.

"Alex," she said, the surprise in her tone not going unnoticed by Raul, her prospective human Happy Meal.

"You know this guy?" Raul asked, pointing to Alex with a manicured finger.

"We're old friends," she said, but even as she did she wondered why she put forth the lie. Alex created too much confusion within her, and she was better off with someone safe like Raul to spend the night.

At her words, her prospective dinner backed away, clearly not about to mess with Alex, especially considering her statement that they knew each other.

Alex slipped beside her, taking one hand in his and placing the other on her waist, establishing a respectful distance. As he did so, she chastised, "It's not good to come between a woman and her—"

"Meal?" he challenged, raising an eyebrow and providing her with a hesitant smile.

"Seriously, Alex. Before you interrupted, I had endured the worst of banalities—"

He placed a finger on her lips. "Can't we just enjoy this dance? Then you can get back to Mr. Chopped Meat."

She snared his finger, yanking it away from her mouth, but with subtle pressure at her waist, he urged her tight to his body.

Stacia didn't battle him, but when she was flush against him, she said, "So I suppose you think you're sirloin compared to my date?"

Alex chuckled and bent his head, totally enjoying the interaction with her. Telling himself that he had approached her just to protect the innocent bystander she had selected for dinner and not because he had experienced an unexpected pang of jealousy at seeing her with the other man. Teasingly he whispered, "More like filet mignon, *querida.*"

She raised her head, a grin on her face. Shifting her mouth toward his neck, she whispered, "Then maybe I should take a nip to see if you're as tasty as you claim."

The graze of her fangs against the side of his throat made his heart skip a beat, waiting for the sting of her bite, but it never came. Instead, she softly whispered, "Don't forget what I am, *amor mío*. How much pain I can cause."

Then she was gone, escaping from his grasp with such speed that he was left standing there, arms held out as if she was still beside him.

Feeling stupid, he dropped his hands and

watched with mixed emotions as she returned to Mr. Chopped Meat, who seemed only too glad to have her back. He suspected that welcome would vanish the moment Stacia sank her fangs into him and the pain she had threatened began.

Alex pulled his thoughts away from them and to the reason he had returned here—to look for Delgado or any of his associates since they had not showed up at Vida Loca, the club where he had met Louie earlier that night

If he could round up enough information, he intended to press for additional DEA agents to help in finding the missing women, breaking up the white-slavery ring and shutting down Delgado's drug operations.

He shot a last glance at Stacia, whose head was bent close to that of her date as she seasoned that night's meal. A twist of jealousy once again tightened his gut, but he drove it away and stayed alert for clues that would help him make his case.

*Honor and duty before all else,* he repeated, too aware of the fact that Stacia seemed to be presenting a challenge to that simple vow.

## Chapter 10

After Alex's report to his boss the next day, Orendain had been satisfied with the preliminary details Alex had managed to put together about the disappearances of the missing women. Coupled with the information that one of the suspects in the possible abductions was also involved in drug dealing, his boss had been willing to assign him a team to help with the investigation.

As Alex walked into the briefing room where the team was meeting to discuss next steps, he took note of the two agents—Samantha Walker and Juan Brock. Walker was pretty in an all-American kind of way. Blonde, lithe and tall, she would eventually be wonderful as an undercover agent on the South Beach scene. With only a few years of experience under her belt, he knew Orendain would make her prove herself before allowing her onto the streets.

Juan Brock was just a few years older than Samantha, but his earlier life had hardened him. A handsome mulatto, he had a rough look to him that fit into any street setting without issue. He had already done one small undercover assignment, but wouldn't be able to get into the high-flying circles Walker would eventually get access to due to her looks and elegance.

Alex stepped to the head of the table and handed the agents a packet with the details he had gathered and a report on his initial observations.

Both opened the folders, and as he laid out the investigation for them, he explained what their respective roles would be.

"I need surveillance at the Widget. I want both of you to man the van while I go undercover inside," Alex said.

Walker immediately jumped in with "If it's women they're after—"

"Attractive women, Walker," Brock teased, but there was no hint of playfulness in his words.

Bristling, Walker replied, "You're not the only one who can go undercover, Brock."

With a shrug of his shoulders, Brock retorted, "Wouldn't want you under my covers, Walker."

"Enough," Alex warned as he leaned on the table, wishing that the animosity between the two would lessen over time. He had worked with them before and they were both bright and capable, but this kind of sniping helped no one.

He turned to Walker first. "It's too soon to send you in. We don't know enough about how they pick the women to grab."

Then he faced Brock. "As for you, the Widget has an upscale clientele. If I need you to back me up inside, we'll have to dress you up a bit."

Straightening, he opened his folder and removed the photos. Tacked them onto the whiteboard at the front of the room as he briefed them in detail and gave them assign-ments to complete before they would both take up spots in a surveillance van.

After he finished, he faced his team. "Do you understand what you're expected to do?"

Although the two glared at each other, it was clear they would do as instructed. Alex knew they would complete their tasks quite capably since Walker and Brock were two of their youngest and brightest.

Ending the briefing, he watched them leave the room and then headed to his own desk to continue working some leads for this case as well as tying up some of the other assignments he had been working while on modified duty.

Those cases had been fairly routine. Noth-ing as complicated or as dangerous as this current assignment. Especially since none of them had involved unbelievably beauti-ful and desirable vampires.

Cursing beneath his breath, Alex forced his mind back to his files and away from Stacia. But way too often, his mind strayed in her direction, and as the afternoon rushed away, his eagerness to see her continued to grow until he finally acknowledged the inevitable.

Stacia had gotten under his skin, and he seemed to have no way to pry her loose.

Her daytime rest was filled with tormented dreams, if one could call those fleeting thoughts in a vampire's sleepless nights dreams.

Stacia was back in Manhattan on that fateful night, the smell of blood and gunpowder all around. The screams of the dying and injured filling the gaps created by the erratic bursts of gunfire.

Ryder was here. She had followed him from his home, wondering where he had gone with such haste.

Now she knew, her vampire sight tracking the blur that was Ryder as he sped up the stairs to a landing where a group of FBI Agents stood poised by a door.

Gunfire from a far rooftop ripped into the agents before Ryder could reach them. When he did, he scooped up the body of one of them and broke through the doorway.

Stacia followed, flying through the air

and onto the landing. Pausing there to gaze within at the sight of Ryder holding a blood-ied Diana in his arms.

That night she had walked right up to them, anxious to know what was occurring, but in her dream she walked past them to the men at the far end of the apartment. Three men, two of whom were dead.

But not Alex.

He lay against the wall, his blood bright against his shirt. Steaming in the cold of the night.

Stacia licked her lips, recalling the taste of that blood. Of his skin, warm and soft, be-neath her fangs.

She raced to his side and knelt before him. He was so weak he lacked the strength to raise his head.

Cradling his chin in her hand, she skimmed her thumb across the rasp of his beard. Brushed away the tears coursing down his cheeks and raised his face.

"You cry for her," she said, her gaze mo-mentarily skipping to where Diana lay in Ry-der's arms, near death.

"I cry for you," he said, trying to raise his hand to her face.

"For me?" she challenged. "I am an elder. I am—"

"Alone," he said, so weakly it was barely more than a whisper.

Anger rose up in her, but not because he dared.

Because he was right.

She was alone. She had been alone for centuries.

But no longer, she thought, leaning toward him, her gaze locked with his as she brushed her lips along the edge of his jaw.

"Do not cry for me, *amor mío*," she said, trailing her lips across his sandpapery-rough skin until she was close to his ear.

"Dead," he said on a long exhalation that was followed by a weak, almost nonexistent breath.

"No, not dead, Alex."

Stacia released the demon and sank her fangs deep into his neck, savoring the flavor of his blood. Continuing to drink until his pulse was but a fragile flutter beneath her lips.

This time she didn't stop. Didn't bestow the kiss that she would later learn had likely saved his existence.

In her dream she kept on sucking until only the barest hint of life remained.

Pulling herself away, she tore open her wrist with her fangs and brought the bloody skin to his lips. Met his emerald gaze and said, "Forever, Alex. This time it's forever."

"No, this is empty," he said, straining to move his head away. Defying her time and time again as she offered herself to him until she finally relented and stopped.

"Why, Alex? Why do you deny yourself?" she asked, unable to believe that he would refuse her.

"Because I want the woman Stacia. I know she's still in there. Still alive," he said, his voice surprisingly stronger. The tears on his face gone along with the wounds on his body.

He rose before her, alive and whole. The chill of the Manhattan night replaced by the Miami sun. Its rays touched her skin, bringing pleasant heat without any pain.

"Alex?" she said as the emptiness within

her slowly receded, replaced by hopefulness. By the promise of possibilities.

"Do not deny yourself, Stacia. The now is far better than any forever," he said and held out his hand.

Stacia popped up in bed, startled by the turn the dream had taken.

For a moment she told herself that her surprise was at the fact that she was dreaming, since it had been so long since she had allowed herself any thoughts during her vampire slumber.

But the heart she had guarded for so long held the truth—her shock stemmed more from the desire that lingered for the mortal in her fantasy. It came from the lightness in her heart that accompanied Alex's invitation to explore life with him.

With her slumber disturbed and the afternoon gone, she rose and walked to the window. Pulled aside the blackout curtains and peered out.

People streamed by below, filled with life. Teeming with happiness and love. Things she had long ago convinced herself were no longer possible for her.

She still wasn't sure that they were, only now she had someone who had managed to challenge those expectations.

When she had showed him weakness, he had responded with kindness.

When she had revealed her demon, he had offered gratitude.

Not what she had anticipated. Because of that, she suddenly had no doubt about what she would do that night.

She would be on the hunt.

Not unusual for a vampire. As a matter of fact, Stacia had done the same thing for nearly two thousand years, but tonight's hunt would be radically different.

Tonight, she would be on the hunt for just one singular man.

With Alex's scent and taste alive in her vamp senses, Stacia left the hotel and tracked him down, speeding from one location to the next until she finally arrived at the Widget. She should have guessed he would be there, she thought as her vamp senses picked up the familiar *lub-dub* of his heart above all the other noise in the club.

"We have to stop meeting like this," Stacia said with a wry smile as she sidled up to Alex at the bar.

Alex barely shifted his gaze her way as he nursed a glass with a slice of lime, mint and clear liquid. Although it looked like a mojito, her vamp senses detected no hint of alcohol. He obviously wanted to keep a clear head while working.

"*Hola,* Stacia," he said, although he continued to look straight ahead, his attention centered on something else.

"*Amorcito,* what can I get you?" the bartender said with a broad smile as he finally approached.

"A mojito," she answered, and despite Alex's less-than-warm welcome, she took a spot at the empty stool beside him. It was empty because she had sent a mental note to the man there to vacate it for her.

Alex finally shot her a half glance, running his gaze up and down her body. "Getting into the whole Miami scene, aren't you?" he said and motioned to the brightly colored floral print of her dress.

"Basic black seems so out of place here,

don't you think?" she replied, trailing a hand along the edge of the dress's bodice, which displayed the ample swell of her breasts. She had picked out the dress earlier that day with him in mind.

His gaze followed the passage of her hand and annoyance flared to life. He had too much to do to be playing footsie with her, Alex told himself even while something else also came alive within him.

"Don't mess with me, Stacia."

She chuckled, noticeably amused. "A warning?"

"Should it be? Are you scared of a mere mortal like me?" he said just as the bartender placed the drink before her.

Scared? She really wouldn't say scared. Intrigued. Restless. Her dreams that afternoon had enticed her into exploring long-unused emotions, as had their meeting of the night before.

Even her late-afternoon attempt at retail therapy had been guided by her desire to test what was happening between them. To see if she could push the boundaries of his control and possibly sample his determined spirit.

But scared?

No, she wasn't going to allow herself to be afraid of a human, dreams notwithstanding.

She picked up the glass and took a sip.

*"Delicioso."* She winked at the bartender, who smiled with pride and walked away without any payment to service another customer.

Alex watched him go and finally swiveled on his stool to face Stacia. "I suppose you just made him think that he got his money."

"A simple enough thing to do," she confirmed with a nod, nonchalant shrug and a sip of her drink.

"Is that how you get everything you want?" he pressed, annoyed by the ease with which she manipulated. Frustrated that she had his full attention. He was responding to her proximity, his body awakening with the recollection of the kiss they had shared the night before.

"Not everything," she surprised him by admitting. Shifting to the edge of the bar stool, she laid a hand on the side of his face and stroked her thumb across the rough beard on his chin. Shifted it upward to trace the edge of his lower lip as she added, "Some-times a challenge is much more…enticing."

Her touch, so simple and tender, did be-guile him. Presented a test he wasn't sure he could pass.

He covered her hand with his and dragged it off his face. Placed her hand on her thigh and, with a paternal pat, tried to communi-cate disdain to fight what he really wanted to do.

"I'm sure you can find someone much more interesting than me to play your little games." He had no time for games that would distract him from his assignment, especially when it was possible the freedom of Dan's daughter and the other women was at stake.

In her many centuries of existence, no one had ever dared such disrespect, Stacia thought. It made her angry, but as it had in her dream, it also fascinated her.

She shifted her hand to his thigh, released only a smidgen of her elder power to show him how she punished those who failed to have regard for her stature. He shuddered be-neath her hand and sucked in a rough breath. The slightly increased beat of his heart further confirmed that her power was working on him.

"You feel that, Alex. I know you do." For good measure, she increased her power and observed, as his body responded, the long, hard length of what was a magnificent erection becoming visible beneath the cotton fabric of his pants. His heartbeat coming ever faster.

She shifted her hand upward until she was so close that a simple movement of her thumb would brush his erection. Although she held off touching him as part of his punishment, for a moment Stacia considered if she was only punishing herself since she itched to explore him. Found her own body wishing for that magnificent erection to fill the emptiness.

At the shift of her thumb against his thigh, his body once again trembled beneath her hand. In a strangled tone, he said, "Stacia, stop it."

"Stop it?" She laughed harshly and said, "You'll have to plead so much prettier than that, Alex."

To her amazement, he mustered the strength

to reach down, cover her hand and say, "Please, Stacia. While you play, another woman might lose her life or her freedom."

He had found her weak point.

She yanked her hand away and released him from her control. Then he surprised her again.

"Thank you," he said, even as he was sucking in a few ragged breaths in an effort to tame his arousal.

Stacia rose and stepped between the V formed by his legs, blocking the view of those in the club as she finally gave in to her desire. She covered his erection with her hand and stroked it, exploring the shape of it beneath her fingers.

"Don't thank me yet, Alex. There is much we still have to share," she said, and with one last caress, she walked away.

Alex's body was shaking with the arousal that had gripped him from her first touch. He swiveled on the stool to face the bar and hide his reaction. *Breathe,* he said to himself, and with several long, steadying breaths he fought his physical response to Stacia. Aware that it would be that much harder to battle the growing emotional attachment to her. With great difficulty, he managed to banish her from his thoughts and returned his full attention to the far side of the club, where a large bouncer stood guarding the entrance to the private rooms.

He had been watching that area since coming into the club, but so far there had been no sign of any of the suspects. But as he sat there, he overheard a conversation down at the far end of the bar. Fragments of a discussion in what he guessed to be Russian.

Earlier that day, the boyfriend of one of the missing women had come out of the coma induced by a severe beating, which had occurred when he had decided to play detective in order to find his missing girlfriend. The injured man hadn't remembered much, but he had recalled that his assailants had been Russian.

Was it too much of a coincidence? Alex wondered, surreptitiously looking down the length of the bar to where three men sat, drinking and laughing amiably. Their dress was average, with no ostentatious jewelry to call attention to them. But as Alex furtively monitored them while also keeping an eye on the entrance to the private rooms, it became obvious that the men had money to spend.

A trio of attractive women, high-priced call girls, he was almost certain, approached the men. In his years as an agent, he had seen enough women like them to recognize professionals. Call it the look in their eyes, hungriness combined with something he could only describe as world-weariness. In heavily accented English, the Russians chatted with the women and paid for a round of drinks and then another. It was then that the man who seemed to be the de facto leader suggested that they see about getting a private room.

The women agreed, and as the men stood, Alex quickly whipped out his cell phone and managed to snap a few shots without being noticed. After his suspects and the call girls left the bar, he emailed the images to his surveillance team with instructions for Brock and Walker to keep an eye out for the six and also to run images of both the men and women through their databases to see if they got a hit.

At the entrance to the private rooms, the group was immediately admitted, confirming to Alex that the Russians had to have some connections based on the ease of their acceptance into the exclusive area. He only hoped money wasn't the only connection that had gained them entry.

Unfortunately, what was happening before his eyes didn't match the earlier patterns of the disappearances. These women were clearly hookers and none of the women who had been kidnapped had criminal records, with the exception of Andrea, who had a couple of juvenile offenses. Also, all the missing women had been much younger than the three working girls who had just gone into the back.

Even with those discrepancies, Alex was concerned for the safety of the prostitutes. They were attractive women and it might occur to whoever was running the white-slavery ring that they would fetch a pretty penny or rate a higher exchange than the one Louie had mentioned. In addition, since many of the prostitutes he had encountered in the past had little family support, they might not be missed by anyone for quite some time if they disappeared.

He wondered if Louie knew if any working girls were involved in the exchanges, which reminded him that he had to go by Louie's apartment to see what his informant had discovered. He had tried calling him several times earlier in the night, but Louie was still not answering, which necessitated the personal visit.

Because of his concern about the working girls, Alex remained at the Widget until nearly closing. Shortly after the call was made for a last round, the working girls emerged from the back rooms, happily chatting and with no sign of the three Russians. They left undisturbed, and although Alex waited until the club started emptying, the three men did not exit the private area via the club.

Forced to leave long after the last call was announced, he exited and walked away from the building and toward Ocean Drive, intent on another mission he had to accomplish that night. As he did so, he called his surveillance team.

"Were you able to use the photos I sent?" he asked as he walked down the side street.

"We've enhanced the images and are going to run them through the system," Walker advised.

"Good job. Did you see the three women leave the club? Anything there?"

"Yes and no. They all got into one car together and drove off. Safety in numbers, I guess. Also, no sign of the men yet," Walker reported.

"Keep an eye out for them. Tell Brock to tail them when they leave and then report back to me." Alex stopped at the corner of Collins, waiting for the light to change. Despite the hour, there was still a fair amount of traffic.

"You've made him a happy man, Garcia. You know he loves any excuse to jump into that tricked-out muscle car of his," Walker said with a chuckle. In the background, he could hear Brock defending himself before Walker playfully said, "Chill, Brock. It's not like I said it's a penis replacement or anything."

"You wish you could ride with me," Brock called out, and Alex chuckled.

"Are you two done fighting?" he asked, both amused and concerned about the antics of his fellow agents.

"We're done. How about you? Are you done for the night?" Walker asked.

"I have a few more stops to make. Reach out to me if there's anything important," Alex said and ended the call.

He continued to Ocean Drive, all the while thinking about Stacia and what had happened earlier that night. About the distraction she presented. Before the night was over, he intended to find a solution to that problem.

But first, he had to pay a visit to Louie's apartment.

## Chapter 11

Stacia had left the Widget determined to find something to satisfy her since playing around with Alex had failed to do so. If anything it had left her more frustrated than ever before.

None of the other noisy clubs along Lincoln Road or Ocean Drive had been appealing, and so she had flown down to the water's edge where it had been too easy to lure one young man to a secluded spot by some small dunes and grab a quick bite.

Immediately after that she had come across

a couple having sex in one of the brightly colored South Beach lifeguard stands.

They had been so involved with each other they hadn't even sensed her presence at first. She had perched on the edge of the stand, a voyeur to the activities, her desire and need mounting along with the couple's. At the moment when the man had been about to climax, she leaped down and sank her teeth into his neck. Sent out a command to the woman to remain still until she was done.

She took the greater part of her feeding from the man before delighting in the woman as dessert. The couple's blood had been laden with their passion, offering her an even greater burst of sexual energy.

With the power of all that life singing through her veins, she had freed the demon to relish the night, racing at superspeed along the water's edge before returning to Lummus Park. At a breakneck pace she had zigged and zagged among the humans occupying the sea walk, passing by unnoticed except for a slight rush of air, which might have seemed like an ocean breeze. Upon reaching the end of the walk, she had sprinted across the street and up to the rooftop of one of the hotels, continuing her blood-fueled dash by leaping from one building to another. Stopping only briefly to admire the neon lights coloring the night and shining their bright hues down on the crowd along the street. Then she watched the parade of cars cruising along the strip until she had flown off again, coming to rest on the rooftop terrace of the Park Central.

As she crouched on the ledge, inhaling the scent of the ocean and the humans below, she considered going back out into the night. But as she stared at the activity below, a disturbing sense of emptiness returned.

The same sense of emptiness she had experienced after her run-in with Alex earlier that night.

With the evening no longer holding any allure, she returned to her room and ordered up a bottle of wine and some food. Although vampires drew no sustenance from either, the taste could be pleasing at times.

Rare times like these where for a short space of time she allowed herself to imagine what it would be like to be human again.

She was halfway through the bottle of wine and had just begun to nibble on the fruits and cheese she had ordered when an insistent knock came at the door.

Puzzlement at the unexpected visit filled her for a second, but as she approached the door, she sensed him. Perceived the whirl of his emotions as Alex stood on the other side of the entrance, waiting for her to answer.

The contradictions were so strong in him that she hesitated, laying her hand on the painted wood of the door in an attempt to discern more.

All she discovered as she centered her energies on him was a maelstrom of conflict. It was so intriguing that it left her with little choice about what to do next.

She yanked the door open and he stood there, one arm leaning against the doorjamb, his other hand tucked into his pants pocket. The position pulled open the fabric of his light blue shirt, revealing a glimpse of his smooth olive skin and deliciously hard muscles. Making her itch to touch him.

Instead, she dragged her gaze to his face, finding some satisfaction in the fact that while she had been checking him out, he had been doing the same.

"How did you know which room—"

"A quick flash of the badge is all it takes. May I come in?" he said, but was moving past her even before she could reply.

She shoved the door shut and tightened the belt on her robe, as if that might somehow armor her against the risk he presented. Why she needed the protection she refused to acknowledge. It took a moment to remind herself that if she wished, she could kill him with a mere flick of her hand.

"What do you want?" she asked, taking a spot across from him at the bistro-size table, which held that evening's simple repast. Not wanting to hope at what his answer would be.

He picked up the bottle of wine and asked, "Do you mind?"

As he had before, he poured the glass without waiting for her reply, which prompted her to angrily snatch the bottle from his hand and smack it down on the table.

"Actually, I do mind, Alex. I really wasn't expecting company and was looking forward to a relaxing night alone," she said, but he ignored her complaint and plopped down into the chair beside the table. Picked up a strawberry from the plate and popped it into his mouth.

He chewed slowly, almost thoughtfully, before he motioned to her with the hand holding the glass of wine. "You and I need a truce of sorts."

"A truce? I didn't realize we were at war," she replied, although, in retrospect, their assorted encounters had clearly created discord between them along with a variety of other sentiments. Sentiments that in part had been responsible for that afternoon's disturbing dream and ensuing hopefulness.

A hopefulness that had been dashed earlier that night when he had ignored her at the bar.

In response to her statement, Alex nodded, raised his glass and took a sip, then leaned back in the chair. His stance was negligently comfortable, although the tangle of his emotions continued to push against hers forcefully. After returning the glass to the table, he idly traced a finger along its lip before he said, "Maybe *truce* is the wrong word.

Maybe *understanding* would be more accurate."

"Understanding?" During her long life, she'd heard more than one man inquire about having an understanding. It had usually related to only one thing. Because of that, she walked around the table to where he sat and insinuated herself into the V between his outstretched legs.

"In all my time, understandings between men and women have invariably been too complicated and, sadly, always detrimental to the woman."

He laid his hands at her waist, drew her deeper into the V even as he sat up. Thanks to the difference in their heights, they were now eye to eye, and there was no mistaking the widening of his pupils or the flush along the high ridge of his cheekbones.

She cupped his jaw and ran her thumb along the stain of color, experiencing the heat of his desire where skin met skin.

"You're diverting my attention at work. That's not a good thing," he said and covered her hand, his palm rough. It had her imagining how delicious that coarseness would be against more sensitive skin. In turn, the nearly imperceptible beat of her elder heart accelerated as the warmth of desire slowly roused her body to life.

"Do you think you're alone in your distraction?" she replied, once again amazed at her abandon with this mortal. During her long life, she had tried to avoid distractions since invariably they proved dangerous. Never had she admitted to a lack of focus, much less one created by a human.

"No, I don't." As if to prove it, he dropped his hand to her neck and encircled one side. Swept his thumb across the increasingly obvious pulse at her throat.

"So what do we do about this, Stacia? How do we go about reaching an—"

"Understanding?"

There was only way that came to her mind.

With shaky hands she slowly began to unbutton his shirt, revealing more of the lean muscles of his chest and abdomen. With a slightly steadier grasp, she grabbed hold of the fabric and parted it. Took a moment to appreciate his masculine beauty. She inched her hands beneath the fabric. Experienced the warmth of his skin as she trailed her hands up to his shoulders and then eased off his shirt, totally exposing his upper body to her gaze.

"This is what I understand," she said as she laid her hands on his shoulders and stroked the broad width. Explored all the hard muscle before dipping her thumbs down to strum the dark brown paps on his pectorals, avoiding the scars on his chest and abdomen from his injuries.

Acknowledging them would have been a too-painful reminder of his mortality. Of the possibilities that had nearly come to an end the night of their first encounter.

"You want me," she said, risking a glance up at his face as she continued to caress him.

"I do want you." Seemingly to prove his point, he undid the belt on her robe and the terry cloth fell loose, exposing a long line of pale, creamy skin to his gaze.

He shifted his hands beneath the fabric to rest on the rounded swell of her hips and inched forward on the seat until his lips were barely an inch from hers.

"But want isn't always good," he confessed, the truth of his words echoing within her.

"We could be quite good together. I think you know that." With one hand she cradled the back of his head, brought her lips to his and exhorted, "Quite good."

He murmured a soft "hmm" and invited her into the kiss, his lips tender as he moved them against hers. His hands soothingly stroking the skin of her waist as he slowly tasted her mouth with his, deepening the kiss by tiny degrees until they were both shaking and barely able to breathe.

Stacia's head was whirling with the sensations he roused with his gentleness. It had been so long since any man had been as tender. Had given her such pleasure with something as simple as a kiss. Which only made her wonder just how much more pleasurable sharing her bed with him could be.

"Alex? What kind of understanding did you have in mind?"

He chuckled and tracked a line of kisses along her cheek, down to her jaw and then to the side of her neck, where he placed a gentle love bite.

She sucked in a breath as her nipples tightened in reaction and he finally said, "Maybe if we explore this attraction, we can find a way to handle it. Be at peace so we can accomplish what we both need to do."

She gave him credit for wording it a little more gracefully than so many others had before him. Nevertheless, it was still the age-old "get it out of your system" rationale, not that she had ever needed such an excuse before to become physically involved with a man.

Of course, in her nearly two millennia of life, she had never been as confused as she was about Alex. About the enigma he presented and the way he had disturbed all that she had thought about herself. About what was possible for the rest of her undead life.

Because of that, she at long last answered, "So let's do what we need to. Let's forge our understanding."

## Chapter 12

"That simple, Stacia? Make love and hopefully learn how to deal with each other?" Alex questioned and pulled back from her, almost not sure that she had really agreed so quickly, but then Stacia repeated it.

"Yes. Let's explore this attraction and find some peace in what we're feeling. Isn't that what you want?"

He wasn't quite sure what he wanted—besides her. But he was certain he had to find a way to temper his response to her so that he could finish his current assignment without additional complications.

But he had never been a man who rushed through anything or gave anything less than his best. This encounter with Stacia would not be any different. If anything, being aware of her past made him want for this time to be totally different for her. To be free of pain and fear.

"What I want," he said, sweeping his hands up her sides until they rested just below her breasts, "is a look. May I?"

Her hands tightened on his shoulders before the tension gradually disappeared. Lowering her hands to her sides, she said, "You may."

Slowly he tracked his hands upward to her shoulders, slipped the robe off them and then ran his hands down her arms, mirroring the fall of the robe. As he reached her hands, he took hold of them in his and appreciated all that his actions had revealed.

She was full-bodied for someone so diminutive. She had perfectly rounded breasts with dark caramel-colored nipples tight with her passion. A narrow waist flared out to generous hips and legs seemingly too long for her size.

At the juncture of those legs, smooth creamy skin.

His erection jerked painfully at the thought of parting those legs and feeling that soft skin against him.

He somehow dragged his gaze upward and met hers. A hint of the demon's blue-green shimmered at the edges of her irises and somehow he knew she was taming the beast to be with him now. Subduing both need and fear.

It was probably not easy for her to relinquish control or give herself freely to someone.

"May I touch?" he said, recalling her troubled past and intending for this to be something much more enjoyable.

"You may," she said and brought their joined hands up to her breasts, where she placed his hands on her. Urged him on with a gentle push and then ran her hands up the length of his arms to rest them on his shoulders.

As tenderly as he had begun his kiss, he explored her, testing the weight of her breasts in his hands before strumming his thumbs across the tight tips. Massaging and kneading them before trapping her nipples between his thumbs and forefingers and rotating them a little more forcefully.

She mewled with pleasure and took a step deeper into the V of his legs, her knees brushing his balls, which were almost painfully hard from his arousal.

He controlled himself, fighting the desire to pick her up in his arms and take her to the bed so he could drive into her. But from the memories she had shared with him, he knew that she'd had little kindness in her life, and he wanted this to be special.

And so he asked, "May I taste?"

His words bounced around in her mind, joining with the myriad emotions Stacia was sensing in him and herself. Dangerous emotions for both of them, entangled as they were in anger and confusion and hopefulness. The latter on her part, at least. But she couldn't deny him, because doing so would be denying herself.

"Please taste," she said, increasing her grip on his shoulders to steady herself as he bent his head and brought his lips to the tip of her breast.

If she had expected haste, she would have been sorely mistaken.

Alex seemed to know only one speed tonight—slow.

Very slow and tender and achingly, immensely pleasurable.

She sighed as he used his mouth on her. Licking. Sucking. Biting. Shifting to her other breast while continuing to caress with his hands, using the moistness left behind by his mouth to ensnare her body and mind.

She was shaking as she cradled the back of his head to hold him near and raised her leg, placing her knee on one side of the chair by his thigh in an effort to be closer.

He whispered against her, "You taste sweet." As if to prove it, he gave a long lick at the tip of her breast and nearly had her coming from the sensation.

"Alex, I need—"

She couldn't finish as he trailed one hand up her leg and stopped at the juncture of her hip and thigh, his thumb brushing across the smooth skin at her center.

"May I, Stacia? May I make love to you?" he said, the tremble in his hands and body confirming that he, too, could no longer wait.

She was afraid to answer, but afraid to refuse, so instead she laid her hand over his. Hesitantly urged his hand down the last little bit to slip his fingers within and find the swollen nub of her clitoris. Press and caress it, causing damp heat to build between her legs.

She closed her eyes against the sensation. Against the sight of him sucking and licking at her breasts. Caressing her clitoris and nether lips until she was at the edge, her body trembling violently. Her arms holding him to her tightly.

When he eased one finger and then another into her, she lost control and came, her body shuddering with the release. The demon surging forward, assuming dominion.

"Alex, *mi amor*," she said, but her words were tinged with the snarl of the vampire.

Alex heard it. Sensed it in the increased heat of her body against his, a byproduct of the monster, he assumed.

As he met her gaze, brilliant blue-green,

and noted the slight show of fang, he asked, "Who will you be tonight, *querida?* The vampire or the woman?"

*The woman, the woman, the woman,* she wanted to shout out, fighting with the demon. Reining in the need to sink her fangs into his smooth skin in order to experience the complete wonder of his arms.

"Stacia?" he questioned again, and she drove back her bloodlust, allowing the human to resume control.

"Make love to me," she said, her voice husky but with mortal need this time.

He surged off the chair then, his arms wrapped around her, and she lifted her legs, encircled his waist as he took the few steps necessary to reach the edge of the bed. Bending his knees, he laid her down on the bed's surface, the fine cotton of the bedspread cool and slick beneath her back as he pressed her down.

As she relaxed, he shifted lower, trailing kisses along her jaw, neck and then back down to her breasts. He teased them with a few loving bites before he placed a line of kisses down her center until he was at the indent of her navel. There he dipped in his tongue, swirling it around before playfully tugging at the golden ring piercing her navel.

Impatiently Stacia arched her back, knowing his intent and welcoming it. Urging him onward.

He didn't disappoint.

His palms were rough as he encircled her thighs and parted her legs. Found the swollen nub at the soft center of her legs with his lips.

She gasped as he loved her, licking and sucking at the sensitive spot. Lowering his head to taste her nether lips before sliding his tongue into her vagina. His thrusts were delicate, initiating her to the rhythm of his loving. As she arched her back higher and cupped the back of his head, her fingers slid through the short strands of his hair.

Finally, thankfully, he eased one finger and then another into her wetness.

Her climax built again, and as much as she wanted to extend the pleasure before her release, she wasn't sure how long she could keep the vampire at bay.

"Alex, I need you. I need you inside me,"

she said, and he must have understood the urgency behind her words.

Rising, he quickly undid his pants and pulled them away together with his boxers, exposing himself.

She had only a moment to appreciate how fine he was. Long, wide and magnificently erect.

Then he filled her, driving deeply on his first thrust. A rough groan escaping him as he held himself there. As he waited for her to become accustomed to the feel of him within her.

Stacia was tight around him, almost as if she were a virgin. So tight and yet slick from his loving and her earlier climax. Warm. So warm that Alex dared a glance to see if the woman was still with him.

She was and he nearly came undone at the beauty of her.

Her dark cocoa-colored eyes were wide and fixed on his face. A very human flush stained the sharp lines of her cheekbones, lessening the starkness of her paleness.

She worried her lower lip with human teeth and he bent his head, licked the spot she had bitten. Whispered a kiss there before he said, "This feels…amazing."

A shuddering breath escaped from her. "It does."

Only the space of another heartbeat passed and then he slowly withdrew, shifted back in. Her tightness caressing him with each stroke. Drawing him closer and closer to his own release.

He closed his eyes, but she cradled his cheek and urged, "Open your eyes. I want to see your eyes when you come."

In truth, he wanted to see hers, as well. Wanted to see that moment when passion reached its zenith and they both tumbled over the edge together.

He did as she asked. Locked his gaze on hers as he stroked in and out, his movements becoming more intense as the pleasure of joining with her grew. As she welcomed him ever deeper, raising her knees to grasp his hips with her thighs. Tightening her grip on his shoulders, her fingernails digging sharply into his skin.

"Alex," Stacia nearly keened, her senses buffeted by the feel of him in her. Above her.

By the smell of his arousal and hers, animal muskiness alive in her nose.

His thrusts pulled her ever closer and she centered her attention on him. On every detail, knowing she wanted to remember this night for some time. That it would bring her solace on the many interminable and lonely nights that would follow long after Alex was gone.

She lost herself in the dark, nearly emerald color of his green eyes, pupils dilated with desire. In the sheen of sweat on the acute planes of his face. The fullness of his lips and the smell of his blood from the accidental nip of her nails into his skin.

The blood summoned the demon to awake. To savor that life force. Yet again she fought the vampire, intent on enjoying a release more satisfying than any she had experienced in centuries.

He didn't disappoint.

With a last few powerful thrusts, he took them over the edge and she fell with him, her body shaking. Every cell of her skin attuned to his. Aware of the nuances of the smooth skin of his chest teasing the tips of her breasts before he lowered himself onto her, wrapped his arms around her and rolled, bringing her to rest on top of him.

She shot him a quizzical look and he shrugged. "I didn't want to crush you."

She refrained from reminding him that she was an elder. She could have tossed him off her with little force. His weight, heavy as it was, had no effect on her physically.

But something kept her from issuing that reminder since the sensation of him, warm, slightly damp with the sweat of their loving and totally human, was just too satisfying. Instead she murmured a sleepy-sounding "Thank you."

"Hmm," he said, and as she laid her head on his chest, listening to his heartbeat as it slowed, he lazily stroked a hand up and down her back.

The gesture was soothing. Loving. It felt natural.

Too natural.

If she hadn't known better, she would say this was something they had done hundreds of times in the past and would repeat again hundreds of times in the future.

Only, he was human and the future was limited for him. The future probably would not even exist if it hadn't been for the night they had met and she had bestowed her kiss on him. A kiss she had not been able to resist because of the love she had seen in his eyes.

She raised her head and propped it up on one hand as she stared down at him, searching his face for that emotion.

It was there, shimmering along the edges of his gaze as it skipped over her face. Longing gripped her hard, making her wish for something that wasn't possible.

"Is something wrong?" he asked, his gaze narrowing.

"Do you remember that night? The kiss?" she asked, wondering. Needing to know if he was aware of her actions during the raid.

As often as the nightmares had come to him, Alex wanted to say that he did remember. That he recalled everything, only the dream always stopped at the same place— just as her fangs grazed his skin and passion overwhelmed him.

"I'm not sure that I do remember everything about that night," he answered honestly.

A long silence filled the room before she finally said, "A vampire's kiss can do many things."

Alex considered her words, his gaze observing every nuance of her features until it finally came to him.

"The bite can make you forget," he said.

Stacia reached up and ran her index finger along his temple and then down to his lips, where the mouth that had just brought her so much joy was now thinned into a harsh line.

She ran her finger across that stark line and replied, "It's why your dreams stop. Because I bit you."

He rolled suddenly, dumping her to the bed. Pinning her body to the mattress while grabbing hold of her hands to keep her from touching him again.

"Why did you do it? Because I was dying and a little taste of my blood wouldn't have made a difference?" His tones were hard, rife with an anger that she understood. He had been powerless and she had taken advantage of that, only…

"A vampire's kiss can also heal. Prolong life if given at the right moment."

An immense shudder worked across his body and he released her. Rose and sat on the edge of the bed, cradling his head in his hands as he contemplated her statement.

She shifted to her knees, watching his back as he sat there. Waiting for his reaction until, with a long inhalation, he finally raised his head and faced her.

"Why?"

One word and yet so many possible responses, she thought for only a second before she blurted out, "Because I had never seen so much love on anyone's face."

Alex shook his head, obviously confused. "But it was love for another woman. For Diana."

"But a heart capable of such love…" She didn't finish, maybe because the answer was evident in his eyes.

"Are you capable of that kind of love?" he asked and laid his hand on the side of her face with such tenderness she nearly wanted to weep.

"Long, long ago, but now…passion is all I can offer," she confessed.

Alex doubted her avowal. As she had hinted at earlier, love did not exist in your heart for only one person or thing. If she had at one time been able to truly love, he suspected she could love once again.

Not that he was interested in that emotion from her.

But for now he would accept the gift she had bestowed upon him—his life—as well as the passion her arms could provide. A passion like none he had ever experienced before.

"I'm willing to share your desire if that's all that you think you have to give," he said and traced his thumb along the edges of her lips.

The smile that came to her face was guarded, as if she suspected there was more behind his offer, but she didn't refuse him.

"Can you stay the night?" she asked.

"I can stay until morning," he confirmed, leaning forward and kissing her once again, inviting her to share what they had both promised to give.

## Chapter 13

Stacia didn't know how many times they had made love during the course of the night. They had all merged together into an incredibly gratifying blur.

She also couldn't remember the last time she had awoken wrapped up in a man's arms. Spooned together, his warm breath slow and soft against the side of her temple. His arm tossed over her waist and the slight stir of his erection along the small of her back signaling that he was awakening, as well.

Had she been human, she might have been sore.

As a vampire she had no such problem and pressed her body back against him, slowly shifting her hips back and forth, fully rousing him.

"Good morning," he said, brushing a kiss along her temple. He reached up, found her nipple and strummed it into a tight peak.

"Is it good?" she replied, not sure it was, no matter how pleasing his touch. The purpose of their night had been to find some way to deal with their attraction. If anything, she worried the appeal had grown even stronger.

"May I show you how good?" he asked and insinuated his knee between her legs, applying slight pressure to create the space he needed to then ease into her vagina from behind.

Stacia sucked in a rough breath, the wonder of him within her more intense than she dared admit. He kept up the gentle caress of his fingers against her breast and then swept his one hand downward, found her clitoris and tenderly pressed against that nub.

"Alex," she sighed, giving in to the pleasure he was bringing her yet again.

"Stacia, you feel too good," he said, his

voice rough as he slowly shifted out of her before driving back in.

Stacia shivered from the friction of his movements and the caress of his fingers between her legs. It was almost more than she could bear, threatening to steal a climax from her before she was ready.

She covered his hand with hers, stilling the motion of his fingers at that sensitive spot.

A second later came the teasing graze of his teeth against the side of her neck, followed by a rough bite. Before she could register his intent, he began to suck at the side of her neck, the pull of his mouth strong. So sharp that she lost control and came, her cry hoarse. Her body shaking forcefully, experiencing a release like no other in the many years of her undead existence.

Her stunning release rolled over him and Alex lost it. He stilled inside her, called her name against the side of her neck. Wrapping his arms around her more tightly, he cradled her, absorbing every nuance of her body. Trying to gentle her with his touch.

Long moments passed before both of their

bodies calmed and he applied gentle pressure, urging her to face him.

When she did he could see the turmoil there. It matched his own. He had wanted to find a way to drive need for her out of his system, but if anything, the sight of her stirred him more now than before. Especially as vulnerable as she looked right at this moment, clearly confused about what had just happened.

"I think you should go," she said, and before he could say anything else, she was a blur of motion. One moment she was beside the bed and the next she was at the door, the robe wrapped tightly around her. Her arms encircling her waist as if she was trying to hold herself from falling into a million tiny pieces.

He slipped from the bed and dressed quickly, sensing it was risky to overstay his welcome.

Even so, he paused at the door, hesitant to leave without saying something. Anything, although he was finding it tough to get the words out.

Haunted emotions hid in the darkness of

her eyes. He hadn't expected that so soon after the pleasure they had shared. Nor did he expect to see the mark of his mouth, vivid against the pale skin of her neck.

He raised his hand and laid his index finger against the already healing bruise. "I'm sorry. I didn't mean to hurt you."

She snagged his finger and eased it away before releasing her hold on him. "I've survived worse, Alex."

"Stacia," he said, hating her upset. Sorry that a night of such sharing and bliss was ending like this.

"This is a mistake, Alex. I think we both know that," Stacia said, reeling from what she had experienced in his arms just moments before. Satisfying, yet frightening. Challenging what she had believed about herself—that she was no longer capable of feeling such joy. Maybe because deep in her heart she knew a release that intense could only happen when coupled with love.

But she was incapable of love, she told herself. Especially love with a mortal man. One who would die and leave her.

One she barely knew.

"Stacia, *por favor,*" Alex tenderly urged, reaching for her once again.

"Go." To make her point clear, she summoned the demon and its power, shoving him out of the room with a forceful wave of her hand.

She shut the door to avoid the look of disbelief on his face. To block the anguish in his eyes and the sight of his mobile lips thinning with displeasure at her actions.

Lips that just minutes earlier had rocked her world, she thought, raising her hand to trace the sensitive spot on her neck. The lightest touch of her fingers weakened her knees with desire before the healing power of the vampire wiped away the final remnants of his loving.

He had put the bite on her.

A mere mortal had dared to mark her.

Only, as she recalled their night together, *mere* was not a word she could use to describe Alex.

With his touch and his kindness, Alex had breached her defenses.

It was something that she could not let happen again, she thought, tightly wrapping her arms around herself once more as the advent of morning summoned her to rest.

She walked back to the bed and slipped beneath the sheets, covering herself snugly.

They smelled of him.

Smelled of their loving.

A big mistake, she thought.

She should bathe to remove those remnants of the night. Change the sheets to avoid him, but the pull of morning was too demanding.

Alex's scent and the warmth of his body lingered in the bed, keeping the chill of the monster at bay for only a scintilla of time before the vampire's slumber claimed her.

Before she fell into dreams, this time of the night they had just shared.

Alex hurried from the hotel, his body sore from the time spent with her. The ache close to his heart possibly more painful, he thought as he rubbed at the spot where he had been shot.

His Crossfire convertible was parked only a block away from the hotel, but he needed time to think about what had just happened and his condo was walking distance.

He hurried down Ocean Drive, his strides long and eating up ground as he considered all that had transpired last night and then this morning.

He had never experienced such gratification before. Such passion. He told himself it was on account of the demon within her. A demon that could control him as if he were no more than a puppet, he thought, recalling how she had tossed him out of her room with a negligent wave of her hand.

But as he walked, the air of a spring morning slightly cool against his skin, he reminded himself that she had been human the entire night. Possibly too human, he thought, remembering the emotions she had revealed to him. The need to be loved that was still alive in her despite nearly two thousand years as a vampire.

He recalled her words about him—that he had a heart capable of great love. Could his heart possibly be capable of loving someone like Stacia? Of loving a demon?

Too quickly the memories came of the

pleasure in her arms. The arms of a woman, because the demon had only emerged this morning when she had begged him to leave.

Leave because she was likely as confused as he was, he thought, clenching his fists. Battling the urge to return to the hotel and ease the torment tattooed on her face.

A bad idea, possibly even worse than last night's idea to get her out of his system.

He had to stop thinking about Stacia. She could take care of herself. In fact, she had been taking care of herself for quite some time before he had come into the picture.

Unlike Andrea and the other missing women who needed someone to take care of them. Who needed him to find them.

With that thought in mind, he crossed the street to his condo. A shower would rid him of the last traces of Stacia and prepare him for the day.

The Russians had left the Widget about an hour after closing.

Brock had followed them back to a cargo ship docked in the Port of Miami. He and Walker were already working on tracing the ownership of the vessel, finding out who was on board and when the ship would leave port. In time he hoped they would have enough probable cause to be able to board and look for evidence.

The search they had conducted through the various American criminal databases had not yielded any hits for the three Russian men. Later this morning they were expanding the search to the databases run by Interpol.

Alex reviewed the short report prepared by his team on last night's surveillance and then viewed the tape, looking for anything they might have missed, not that he expected that. Brock and Walker were good agents whom he trusted. They had not let personal feelings get in the way of their work.

Unlike he had done on occasion over the past few days.

An hour later, after fast-forwarding through the tape, he confirmed that there had been nothing out of the ordinary during the course of the night except for the presence of the Russians.

Finishing the ice-cold dregs of his Cuban

*café con leche*, Alex decided to try to reach Louie again. He had passed by Louie's apartment that morning on his way to work, but no one had been home.

It was worrisome that his informant hadn't called and was nowhere to be found. Even when Louie didn't have any information, he was always one for keeping Alex up-to-date on what was happening along the Ocean Drive strip and the nearby locales.

He again dialed Louie's number using a secure and unlisted phone number at the agency. The cell phone rang and rang. Alex was just about to hang up when someone answered.

Not Louie, but it was nevertheless a familiar voice.

"Is that you, Black?" Alex asked.

"It is," the Miami Beach P.D. lieutenant answered.

Definitely not a good sign that the police department had a hold of Louie's cell phone.

"Where are you?"

Black immediately answered, "The morgue."

Nope, definitely not good, Alex thought.

## Chapter 14

Alex stared at Louie's naked body on the stainless-steel table of the medical examiner. An assortment of bruises marked Louie's torso, but the worst of the damage was on his head and hands. Half of his face was caved in from the beating, and it looked as if most of his fingers had been broken. But despite the damage to his visage, it was clearly Louie. The familiar rose tattoo between his thumb and forefinger on his right hand further confirmed his identity.

"You can save us some time by identifying the body," Lieutenant Black said as he stood beside Alex and gestured to the corpse.

"Luis Alvarado. Small-time drug dealer. One of my informants," Alex replied, bending to examine the assorted wounds on Louie's body. The bruises had a decided pattern to them, as if they had all been made by the same weapon. Even his face showed some of the same markings. He turned his attention to Louie's fingers. They were smashed to bits and the damage was so extensive that he couldn't tell if the injuries had been made by the same weapon as the other bruises.

"Was he working for you?" Black asked as he slipped on latex gloves and eased Louie's face to one side.

Alex nodded, straightened, and Black said, "Do you think he blew your cover?"

With those kinds of injuries, anything was possible. He was going to have to advise his team of the potential breach of security so they could be vigilant for their own safety and watch his back more closely while he was undercover at the clubs.

"Possibly," he said and continued with his scrutiny since something about the wound patterns looked familiar. "Can you get me photos of these injuries right away?" he said and motioned to several distinct contusions along Louie's ribs and arms.

Black bent to look at the damage. "Am I missing something?"

Alex pointed to the unique pattern of the wounds. "I thought I saw something similar on the photos of the missing woman's boyfriend's body when they brought him into the E.R."

Black examined the injuries again, focusing more closely on the design this time. "Could be. I'll have the M.E. send the pictures to you ASAP. Do you think this is connected to the case you're working?"

"It's too coincidental not to be related to the investigation. Louie was supposed to put me in touch with the suspects. Where did you find him?" Alex asked, continuing to work his way around the corpse, looking for any additional clues.

"Worker at the Watson Island Park noticed something at the edge of one of the parking lots. Beneath the overpass for the MacArthur Causeway."

"You found the missing woman's boy-friend across the way, right? By the far end of the Parrot Jungle Trail," Alex commented as he once again straightened from the table and faced Black.

"We did," Black confirmed.

"My team followed a trio of Russian men to a ship docked in the Port of Miami."

The police lieutenant quickly made the connection. "If they're driving to the Port of Miami from South Beach—"

"They would go past both locations on a regular basis. That's too much coincidence for me," Alex said.

"Me, too. Can you put a full-time tail on them?" Black asked, but Alex shook his head.

"I don't think my boss will go for that. He's not sure there's anything going on here that warrants DEA attention. If something doesn't happen with my investigation soon, he's likely to pull the plug on the operation."

Black nodded and glanced down at the body. "I'll see what I can do, but it may not be easy. Without a direct connection to the assault on the boyfriend and the missing women, this is just another routine homicide."

Frustration colored the other man's voice and Alex understood it well. They were always working understaffed and underfunded by the government. Oftentimes they were also outgunned by the criminals they were trying to capture.

He clapped Black on the shoulder. "You get me the photos. Maybe we'll be able to piece enough together to keep this investigation going and get the manpower we need on the case."

Black nodded. "Whatever you need, Garcia. I'm not happy with the thought of our girls being shipped overseas as slaves."

Stacia awoke with a hunger far stronger than any she had experienced in some time.

She drained two of the blood-bank bags she had in the refrigerator, but they failed to fulfill her need.

She was about to drain a third but realized that she would not be satisfied with cold blood. She needed the heat of the energy from a living, breathing meal. An up-close-and-personal kind of feeding to end the hunger twisting her insides into knots.

Unfortunately, the afternoon sun was still too potent for her to emerge from the hotel, but she was incredibly thirsty and couldn't wait any longer. There had to be patrons mingling about the lobby or in the restaurant. But first she had to be ready to snare someone.

Which meant removing Alex's scent from her body.

Determined to also cleanse him from her mind.

She showered, then perused her closet. Since she was heading downstairs and didn't want to attract too much attention, she kept her outfit simple—black jeans and a cropped black T-shirt that showed off the golden ring at her navel.

Unfortunately, the sight of that ring in the full-length mirror brought to mind Alex's playfulness of the night before and the sweet tug of his mouth.

She drove those thoughts from her mind and escaped her room, intent on finding sustenance.

Luck was on her side much as it had been the afternoon before.

There were two men at the lobby bar— one blond and one brunet. She opted for the blond, thinking he would make a welcome change from all the Latinos she had savored over the past few days.

From Alex.

She sat at the bar, leaving an empty chair between herself and her target. Ordered a glass of red wine and sent out the first little wave of elder power. It usually worked like chum cast on the ocean, ensnaring men in her net of desire, not that she had really needed it this time.

She'd had the man's attention from the moment she sat down, but there was still something satisfying about proving the strength of her vampire power. About knowing she could control humans with the barest use of her force.

The nagging voice in her head reminded her of how unfulfilling this encounter might be. How an assignation with Alex was far better, only this was her life. Her undead reality. It was the way she had survived for hundreds and hundreds of years, and she wasn't about to let one puny mortal make her feel guilty about it now.

Nor was she about to hope for something different.

With a powerful blast of her power, she reined in her companion, forcing him to rise and follow her from the room. As they walked out, she asked, "What's your name?"

"D-D-ennis. D-Dennis from Ohio," he stammered, slightly dazed from the strength of her possession.

Stacia smiled, a sly smile that didn't reach her eyes. "Well, Dennis from Ohio, we are going to have some fun."

A grin that approached a leer erupted on Dennis's face as he held up the key to his room.

"I'd like that," he said.

Stacia tore the key from his hand and, with an elegant flutter of her fingers, pulled him along toward his room.

Dennis from Ohio lay stiffly on the bed. Not dead but empty of any feeling. Devoid of any emotion from the passion he had just experienced thanks to her vampire kiss.

Just as she was feeling nothing.

No satisfaction, only guilt.

Even her blood hunger lingered, as if the impressive quantity she had taken from Dennis hadn't been enough to satisfy the void within her.

She rushed to the bathroom and cleaned away the traces of the encounter.

After she finished washing her mouth and hands, Stacia braced her hands on the edge of the sink and stared into the mirror.

Nothing stared back and maybe that was better.

She didn't want to see the emotions on her face. Didn't want to see if her eyes were as vacant as those on poor ol' Dennis from Ohio.

She feared they would be. She worried at the gnawing need deep in her center that hadn't been slaked by taking the young man.

She blamed it not on Alex but on the fact that she hadn't fed enough.

That was the reason she still hungered.

Returning to the room, she walked to the

window and peered outside. In the hour or so since she had roused from her vampire respite, the afternoon sun had begun to wane. Now it was low enough in the sky that she could venture outside and obtain someone else to end the craving within her.

With barely a glance at Dennis, she fled the room, avoiding his uncomprehending stare. Telling herself that when he woke, he would thank her for the pleasure he had experienced. Or at least what he remembered of the pleasure, since her bite would erase large parts of his memory.

With haste in her steps, she exited the hotel and cruised the Ocean Drive strip, wanting to find another meal and encountering only frustration. While there were dozens of humans strolling around, it was still too early for her to just take a bite of someone without resorting to elder power to lure them to a discreet location. She was too impatient for that right now, but curbed her frustration, reminding herself that recklessness led to problems. In her extended existence she had known more than one vampire who had lost their life because they had chosen the wrong person at the wrong time.

Her restraint had kept her from such an end.

So she bided the tug of need within her and ambled along the Lummus Park path, savoring the soft sea breeze blowing westward. Taking a moment to watch the children having fun in one of the playgrounds.

They reminded her of her younger brothers and sisters, long since dead. Their faces and voices only faded memories in her brain, much like those of her parents. Even Cassius's empty face was blurry in her mind, although his actions would remain with her always.

The hunger within her grew as she lingered close to the children. Viewed the carefree happiness they exhibited and which she had not known in so long.

Until a tiny voice reared up inside her and reminded her of last night. Of this morning.

Reminded her of all that she had experienced with Alex.

All that she could not have.

She whirled from the playground and back

to the path. The sun hung low in the sky, brushing the horizon with its bloodred hues. She lounged on the seawall and waited, delaying until the edge of the bright orange-red sun touched the sea.

Long ago she had overheard a father telling his son that if he listened carefully, he could hear the sea sizzle as it extinguished the sun's heat.

She listened, opening herself up to the world around her. Her vampire senses picking up every nuance of man and creature in the immediate area. The rustle of the palms and rush of the waves against the shore. The distant shouts of some beach volleyball players finishing up a game.

She waited, but there was no sizzle as the sea swallowed up the sun, providing her greater freedom to find sustenance. To end the need within her that feeding from Dennis had not fulfilled.

With the demon's power burning through her veins, she rushed to the beach, allowing herself to race along the surf's edge as she relished the eruption of night. Sought out what would fulfill the vampire.

Long minutes passed before she felt it safe to snag one young man as he slipped into the gap between two condos built along the beachfront. She grabbed hold of him and dragged him into the shadows by one building.

The skin of his neck was salty from the ocean. His body still damp and slightly cold as he had clearly just come from a quick dip. She fed on him with no preliminaries, sinking her teeth deep and draining him until she knew she had to stop.

He crumpled to the ground and she placed him up against the wall. Anyone passing by would think he'd had a bit too much to drink, and when he roused, so would he from the blood-loss hangover.

She returned to the water's edge, hunger still driving her.

The thrill of the hunt shoved away the emptiness as she brought down another young man—a skimboarder—and after him a bodybuilder who was doing a few final push-ups at one of the weight stations in the sand.

Gorged with blood, her head whirled as a rare giddiness swept over her. She hadn't experienced anything like it in thousands of years, not since she had first been freed of Cassius's imprisonment and had taken out her anger on various victims.

She had to burn off some of the excess energy to restore balance, and released herself to the night, sprinting up and down the beach before heading toward Ocean Drive. There she did the same, flashing past the hotels with their glaring neon lights and restaurants clamoring for patrons with their curbside hostesses.

She kept at it until she was at the easternmost edge of Lincoln Road. She turned and headed up through the pedestrian mall, weaving through the crowds. Expending energy until some measure of balance had occurred, although she was still slightly light-headed from her gluttony when she finally stopped near the end of the mall.

A dance, she thought. A dance would help burn off the last of it, and luckily, she was only a block away from the Widget.

She ignored the voice in her head warning that Alex would be there. She didn't care that he would be. Hell, she might even put the bite on him and attempt to exorcise the feelings he had roused in her.

Briskly walking to the Widget, she ignored the bouncer's displeased glance at her too-casual apparel, dismissively flicked her hand at him and earned immediate entrance to the club by her mental decree. She disregarded the loud grumblings of the patrons in line, as well as their musings as to whether she was some kind of celebrity to warrant such treatment and dress.

If they only knew, she thought, and aimed straight for the dance floor, where she began to gyrate to the beat of the music. It was loud and rough, matching the way she was feeling. She danced until some of the high from the blood faded, but as she glanced around, she realized that in her earlier state, she had let loose some of her elder power. It had been an attractant for the men surrounding her, eager to have a go.

Maybe later, she thought, and engaged herself in the dance once again.

Alex had caught her entrance earlier that night in the periphery of his gaze. There had been something immediately different about her besides her casual dress. Something almost reckless as she went straight to the dance floor and released herself to the music.

He had tried to ignore her but only half accomplished that. Unluckily, none of his suspects had appeared that night, making his job both easier and harder.

Easier because it let him keep an eye on Stacia.

Harder because it meant he would likely get no information tonight to help him solve the case.

When they made the announcement for last call, he advised his team on what to do and was about to leave when he realized trouble was brewing with Stacia on the dance floor.

One of the men who had gone to her side earlier had sidled up to her, intimately pressing against her. He watched as she shifted away, clearly uninterested in the advance, but the man pressed close once more.

Stacia was a combination of grace and sex as she moved. But there was no denying her growing anger as the man dared to approach yet again. He could feel her ire, and as he noticed that her gaze was growing brighter with the vampire's light, he had no doubt that he had to intercede.

He quickly slipped onto the dance floor and insinuated himself between Stacia and the man. When the interloper would have protested, Alex shot him a threatening look.

Since Alex had several inches and a bit more muscle on the man, he backed away.

As Stacia finally turned to see who had dared to touch her, eyes blazing with the demon's blue-green sheen and a low snarl escaping from her lips, he immediately said, "Not happy to see me?"

Recognizing he had taken the place of her erstwhile Lothario, her demeanor instantly relaxed. With a chuckle, she said, "He's lucky you stepped in."

"But will I be lucky?" he teased, easing his hands to the bare skin exposed at her waist.

"Noway, nohow," she answered with a surprisingly girlish giggle at the end.

He bent down and examined her more closely. Noticed the odd glitter in her eyes and the high color along her cheeks. She seemed oddly animated as he moved with her as she continued to dance. If he didn't know better…

"Are you drunk?" he asked, although he detected no scent of alcohol on her breath. Nor of any other substance, luckily.

"Not in the human way, *mi amor*," she responded playfully and leaned against him, raised her hand and cradled his cheek.

In a vamp way? he thought and wondered just what that entailed for only a moment before concern set in.

He covered her hand with his and yanked it away from his face. "Just how many drinks did you have tonight?"

She pulled her hand out of his and then started to count down on her fingers, her movements slightly disjointed. "Let's see. There was Dennis from Ohio and a nice beachgoer. Then there was—"

"Let's go," he said, roughly grabbing hold of her hand and dragging her through the crowd until they were outside. Even when she stumbled, he pressed her onward until they were at his car. "Get in."

Surprisingly she did as he asked with no argument. Once he was seated, she offered up her hands as if to be restrained and said, "Are you going to take me in? Do you want to handcuff me?"

When he didn't answer right away, she added with another uncharacteristic giggle, "Handcuffs can be fun, you know."

"You *are* drunk."

"Maybe I have had a little too much. I need to burn off some of this blood energy to clear my head," she admitted as it finally occurred to her how she was behaving.

"Some fresh air might do you good, as well," he said and pulled away from the curb, needing a clear breeze also to control the heat of his anger at her actions.

How many had she hurt? he wondered, and then a more sickening concern came to him.

Had she killed anyone in her diminished state? he worried as he drove down Collins and toward the causeway. Keeping a close eye on her, he continued on the highway until he reached the road toward Key Biscayne, the night air blowing in since he had the top down. The rush of air was refreshing until he finally pulled into the parking lot for one of the Key Biscayne beaches.

The lot was empty. Just what he needed to deal with his troublesome passenger.

Her head was tilted back against the seat and her eyes were closed. Her mouth was open slightly and slack, giving the appearance that she had fallen asleep. When a soft snore escaped her lips, it made her seem decidedly too human until he reminded himself of why they were here.

She didn't rouse as he left the driver's seat, came around and opened her door. Nor did she move when he slipped his arms beneath her, picked her up and walked with her to the water's edge.

Unmindful of the wet on his dress slacks and shoes, he continued until the water was about knee-deep.

Heaving her slightly higher, he then let her fall.

The waters swallowed her up, but then she shot upward immediately, soaking wet, with her eyes all glowy and long, lethal fangs exposed. A low growl emanated from her lips as she glared at him.

A split second later he was flying through the air and up onto the sand where he landed with enough force to drive the air from his lungs. She was instantly upon him, straddling his legs with hers. Snaring his hands and pinning him to the sand.

"Why did you do that?" she snarled, water dripping onto his face from the soaking-wet strands of her short dark hair.

"Thought you might need to clear your head." He smiled at her, attempting to disguise his fear.

She jammed his hands deeper into the sand. "Do you know what I am? What I can do to you?"

"Haven't you done enough of that already? Killing? Turning people?" he challenged, the vehemence of his words catching her by surprise, so much so that he was able to reverse their positions and pin her to the sand.

Stacia could have easily tossed him off, but the weight of his body was pleasant. His insinuations weren't.

"I haven't killed or turned anyone for hundreds of years, maybe longer," she explained.

He considered her, glancing at her intently, and his hold finally loosened.

"But you fed tonight. Repeatedly."

She shrugged, unperturbed by his claim. "It's what we do. It's the only thing that gives me pleasure."

Relief washed over him a second before a wicked grin erupted on his face. His eyes gleamed with determination as he said, "*Querida,* we both know that's a lie."

"You're so wrong about that," she retorted, unwilling to admit to how he affected her.

He bent his head, and in that barest breath of time, she morphed back to her human state. Nuzzling her nose with his, he whispered, "Dare me to prove you wrong."

Dare him? she thought. Sweet Lord, she couldn't resist the challenge. "I dare—"

His lips were on hers before she could finish, proving the lie. Rousing her desire—her human desire. Igniting need that, if she admitted it, was far stronger than the demands of the vampire.

She cradled his head close, returning the kiss. Tasting him much as he sampled her.

"You taste like ocean," he said, as she opened her mouth to him.

"I swallowed half of it when you dunked me," she playfully reminded, and was thankful for it lest he possibly taste something far more revealing.

He eased his tongue into her mouth, danced it across hers and the fine straight line of her teeth. Continued kissing her until both of them needed more. She exerted pressure and he understood, flipping to his back so she could straddle him once again.

Stacia released his hands and he immediately put them at her waist, inched beneath the sodden fabric of her T-shirt to reach up and cup her breasts. She sighed with pleasure as he rotated her nipples between his thumbs and forefingers, each twist creating a knot of need within her.

Suddenly a light flashed across her body. Sweeping back and forth, back and forth. The sound of car tires crunching on the pavement, and the growl of a powerful engine intruded.

A park police car had pulled into the lot. The driver aimed a spotlight mounted on the door in their direction, swept the beam of light across their bodies once again.

"Go away," she said, sending a blast of elder power toward the police cruiser. The light snapped off and the driver of the car did as she asked, but the moment seemed shattered, since Alex pulled his hands back down to her waist.

"Alex?" she questioned, wondering at his withdrawal.

"It's wrong like this, like some cheap hookup," he said, tempering his words with the gentle whisper of his hands across the bare skin of her midriff.

*A cheap hookup,* she repeated mentally, thinking of all she had already done that night. Guilt slammed into her as she thought of poor ol' Dennis from Ohio. Of the others who hadn't even had the pleasure before the pain.

She started to move off him, aware that their night had come to a frustrating end, but then he startled her by saying, "Come home with me."

## Chapter 15

Home, she thought. With him?

She hadn't had a home in she didn't know how long. The past three years she had spent in Manhattan had been the longest span of time she had lived in one city for centuries.

*Come home with me,* she repeated mentally and told herself not to make more of his invitation than what it was.

He only wanted a more comfortable place to continue their tryst.

"I'd like that," she said, and in a flurry of movement, they were rising from the sand and heading back to his car.

At the vehicle, he popped open the trunk and pulled out a beach towel, offering it to her.

"So you don't get a chill."

"Vamp," she replied, since chill was a standard part of her nature.

He offered it again. "Okay, so how about you do it to spare my leather seat from the sand and water?"

"Typical guy," she teased, but when she reached for the towel, he stepped up to her and wrapped it around her, his actions full of caring. The tender brush of his hands as he tucked the towel tight reviving the confusion she had been feeling all day.

"Why are you doing this?" she wondered aloud, tilting her head up to gaze at his face.

His own turmoil was evident. His amazing green-eyed gaze was troubled as he shook his head. "I wish I knew why. All I know is that it feels right."

Not the most romantic of answers and yet about as truthful as they came.

"Okay," she replied and slipped into his car, the towel wrapped around her wet and sandy body. It did offer protection from the increasing chill as they drove along the causeways, the night air rushing across them. The star-filled sky bright above as they rode in the open convertible.

His home wasn't far, just up and over the MacArthur Causeway and south of her hotel in the South Pointe section.

He pulled into a parking lot in front of a tall condo building nestled close to the water. Alex came around and helped her from the seat of the low-slung car. She accepted his gallant offer, wrapping her arm around his as they walked to the door of the building and entered. Strolled together like any other couple ending the night, only her nights didn't normally end like this.

His unit was ten floors up, and once they were within, she realized the height of the apartment, coupled with the location of the building, gave him marvelous views of the ocean, Fisher Island, the Government Cut, which housed the Port of Miami, and some glimpses of downtown Miami.

"Beautiful." She sighed, appreciating the sights. Along the port, the lights from a number of cruise ships brightened the night. Farther beyond were the illuminated buildings of the city.

"Very beautiful," he said, coming up behind her and slipping his arms around her.

He was so much larger that he surrounded her with his embrace. It was a comforting feel, but she didn't allow herself to imagine it could be anything more than a passing moment in her too-long life.

With gentle pressure, he urged her around until she was facing him. Cupping her jaw, he bent and brushed a kiss across her lips before he said, "Why don't we get cleaned up?"

"Sounds good," she replied.

"Bath or shower?" he asked, still in solicitous mode as he slipped his hand into hers and led her deeper into his condo.

"Shower," she immediately answered. Since Cassius, she hadn't been a big fan of combining men and baths. Besides, she didn't think she had the patience to wait for a bath to fill in order to be next to Alex.

"I couldn't wait that long, either, so a shower it is," he said with a chuckle and finished leading the way.

The bathroom was sumptuous with a large

Jacuzzi tub and an even larger shower. She waited by its sliding glass doors as he fiddled with the knobs and got the water going. Then he turned to her and grasped the ends of the towel and tossed it away. Slowly and gently helped her remove the rest of her sodden clothing until she stood naked before him.

He was about to reach for her, but she playfully slapped his hands away. "Not fair."

Arching a brow, and with a devilish twist to his lips, he took off all his clothing. Tardily. Making the removal of each garment into a delicious striptease.

He was magnificent, she thought, admiring all the lean, sculpted muscle and the very obvious proof of his arousal. Dismayed by the scars that ruined his olive skin and were too vivid a reminder of his mortality.

Risking a glance at him, she realized he was making no move to touch her, which puzzled her until he said, "Is your head clear now?"

"Yes," she advised, nodding and reaching up to lay a hand in the middle of his chest.

At her answer, he took a step closer, until the jut of his erection brushed against the soft skin of her belly. He laid one hand on her waist and skimmed the line of her collarbone with the other.

"That's good, because I want you to know what we're doing. I want you to remember each and every second of it," he said, but there was a harshness to his words at odds with the gentle way he held her.

Intuitively she understood. Knew there was a war going on within him, which matched her own conflict.

"I'll remember," she said, and he dipped his head, took her hand into his and led her into the large shower.

Bone-melting hot water came at them from all sides, chasing away the last remnants of the nip from the ride in their wet clothing. Ridding her skin of the cold so that when he wrapped his arms around her and drew her close, nothing of the beast remained outwardly.

He held her for long moments, basking in the heat of the water before he reached with one hand toward a dispenser on the wall and pumped something into one hand. At her questioning glance, he said with a smile, "You don't want to rush, do you?"

She was used to taking, used to the haste created by the demon's need. Something very different obviously beckoned on this night.

"No hurry. I have forever, remember?"

Her words transformed his smile into a grim line, but he pressed onward, bringing his hand to her head, where he worked shampoo into her hair.

The shampoo had a clean, citrusy scent. The kind of fragrance a man would use, she thought as he brought up his other hand and massaged the lather through the short strands of her hair. His fingers pressing into her scalp with a sensuous massage.

She moved her head back so she could watch him as he worked, his face intense. The actions of his hands deliciously relaxing, dragging an almost purr from her.

"That feels good," she said.

"Close your eyes. I need to rinse out the soap."

Trustingly she did as he asked, following the tender request of his hands as they came to her shoulders and shifted her backward, directly under one of the showerheads to rinse her hair, and then turned her back toward the center of the shower.

As she opened her eyes, she realized he had grabbed a washcloth, and once again he pumped something onto its surface.

"Turn around," he said, and she did.

A second later came the soapy caress of the washcloth against her shoulders before he shifted it all across her back. Down to her ass, along the backs of her thighs before he moved to her shins and slowly, achingly, worked his way back up.

Her heart was pounding in her chest, her breath ragged as he ran the washcloth across her abdomen. Dipped it into the indent of her navel. Swept it swiftly to her breasts where he took his time, circling each breast with the rough, soapy washcloth. Brushing the hard tips with it until she was shaking and her knees were so weak she had to brace her hands on the wall of the shower for stability.

"Alex," she protested, reaching behind her and trailing her hand along the tip of his erection, needing him to fill her and satisfy the ache his ministrations had created.

"Forever, remember?" he whispered against the shell of her ear as he dropped one hand down and brought the washcloth to the smooth skin at the juncture of her thighs.

She parted her legs, allowing him to slip his hand within. The washcloth was slick and abrasive against her nether lips as he stroked it along her most private areas.

She murmured a protest and pressed back against him, the soap on her body letting her slide freely across his erection, but he brought his other hand down to her midsection and stilled the motion.

"Not yet, *querida,*" he urged and tossed aside the washcloth, moving her just a few inches closer to a showerhead where he rinsed off the soap. Used his hands to direct a soft jet of hot water to the sensitive nub of her swollen clitoris.

Her body was primed for him. Aching, but she held back, engaged by his little game. Wanting her own chance to explore every inch of him.

Facing him, she said, "It's my turn."

Alex smiled and watched as Stacia dispensed some shampoo into her hand, but with his nearly foot more in height, she needed his assistance.

"Kneel," she said, a regal tone in her voice and tilt to her head that he assumed she must have used quite often in her earlier life as a Roman senator's child.

"I'm at your command," he teased back, bringing a grin to her face.

As he knelt, he grabbed hold of her thighs, running his hands up and down the water-slick skin as she shampooed his hair. Her hands massaging his scalp. His face pressed against her midsection, where he dropped a kiss on her belly and then played with the golden ring at her navel.

"Close your eyes," she said, repeating his earlier words, only she didn't reposition him. Instead, she cupped her hands and sluiced water over him time and time again until the shampoo was gone.

He heard the pump of the soap dispenser once again and then her hands were on him, spreading the lather across the width of his shoulders. Dipping down across the muscles of his chest. She paused by the scar, running her thumb along newer skin that was still sensitive to the touch.

"Did it hurt much?" she asked and met his gaze.

"Not as much as the pain that came after," he answered and raised his hand to rest it by the spot on her neck where he had bitten her. Imagining the pain of another bite and the loss of her life.

She skimmed her hand over his, her palm soap-slick before she moved her hand down his arm. She finished lathering up his chest and then urged him to rise where she soaped up the rest of him, avoiding the one place where he wanted her touch more than anything.

To reach his back, she leaned close, the tight tips of her breasts swaying along the wall of his chest from the motion of her hands as she massaged the lather into his back. Then she was urging him beneath the streaming water.

When he was done, she stepped from the shower and held out her hand, inviting him to follow.

They dried each other off slowly, the strokes

gentle on their bodies but increasing their mutual need.

Still they delayed, moving leisurely toward his bedroom. Taking their time as they eased into bed and kissed.

Alex thought he would go insane from the want of her, and yet he couldn't get enough of her lips and mouth. Of the feel of her body, still warm from the shower, wrapped tightly to his. When he finally couldn't bear another moment, he tenderly brought her thigh over his, slipped between her legs and slid inside.

A long, satisfied sigh came from her, and he waited, savoring her tightness and the wet of her. Loving the way she welcomed him with her arms and mouth and the slick caress of her vagina.

He was trembling when he finally moved, his strokes slow and tender. His body pressed tight to hers while he continued to kiss her, all the time thinking that it was crazy that it felt so right. That he couldn't possibly be making love to a vampire and seriously thinking about forever.

Stacia sucked in a breath as one of his strokes nearly took her over the edge. She battled back her release, wanting this moment to never end. Imagining that a lifetime of nights like this were possible with him, only...

He was a mortal.

And she couldn't keep him from the life he was meant to live, because sorrowfully, she knew what it was like to lose all those possibilities.

The sadness that enveloped her loosened her tenuous grasp and she climaxed, calling out his name. A tear escaping as he lost control with her, uttering her name with heartbreaking caring.

It had been too long since she had heard such a thing. Since she had experienced satisfaction of both body and mind.

He wrapped his arms around her, his erection still tucked into her, and whispered, "Rest, *querida*."

She didn't need to rest, but she didn't want to leave the peace of his arms.

Her head against his chest, she closed her eyes and allowed the vampire to emerge only long enough to memorize everything about him. His scent, manly and with a hint of citrus from his shampoo and body wash. His shape, large and protective as he surrounded her. The feel of him, hard muscle and smooth skin. Finally, the beat of his heart, growing slower as sanity returned.

When he slipped from her body as his erection ebbed, she made a motion to rise, but he gently grasped her waist and whispered, "I don't want you to go."

As she met his green-eyed gaze, she saw no deception there. Nothing to say his words were untrue or self-serving.

She flipped and spooned herself against him. Enjoyed the weight of his arm as it wrapped around her waist. Counted each heartbeat and breath until she was certain he was asleep.

Then and only then did she ease from his side.

She stood and watched him sleep for quite some time, standing as still as a statue beside the bed.

Imagined watching that every night, only she knew it was not meant to be.

Whatever was happening between them, as pleasurable as it was, could not be. She had nothing she could offer him and so much more she would take from him.

Because of that, she fled into the night.

Alex came alert at the sound of a door opening and closing.

Stacia was gone.

He laid his hand on the mattress in the space where she had been earlier in the night. He rubbed the sheets, finding them rough compared to the silk of her skin. Holding on to the memory of the feel of her because he suspected that was all he would have in the future.

Memories.

He had expected that she would run despite his entreaty.

Hell, if she hadn't run, he might have eventually come to his senses and done so, although that would have been difficult since it was his home.

A home that he had not ever shared with another woman because none had been special enough for such an event.

Flipping onto his back, he rubbed his fingers across the scar on his chest. Fresh desire rose as he remembered her touch there, but then he recalled his words to her about the emotional agony that had followed.

When he'd been shot, the pain after had been so much greater than just the physical discomfort, because in those seconds as his life faded away, he had become aware of all that he had not done. Of all that he would lose when death claimed him.

Had she felt the same way? he wondered.

In those last moments of life before she had become a vampire, what had she felt? And what did she feel now?

She had told him that the only pleasure she experienced came from feeding, but masculine pride rose up and said she had certainly experienced gratification with him more than once in the past few days. More importantly, they had crossed a line tonight.

A dangerous and fragile line because they had both enjoyed satisfaction of a different kind—emotional satisfaction.

He hadn't expected it.

Had pretty much written off ever feeling anything like it again once Diana had dumped him in New York City that last time. And for Ryder Latimer, one of the undead.

But maybe now he understood what his ex-lover experienced in her vampire's arms.

That didn't make his current situation any easier.

He was emotionally involved with one of the undead and he didn't know what to do about it.

Pulling the pillow on which she had rested her head close, he inhaled deeply and her scent filled his senses. He closed his eyes, allowed himself to imagine all the possibilities and impossibilities until a troubled sleep finally claimed him.

## Chapter 16

Stacia ran as if a hell dog was after her, sprinting along the hard-packed sand at the water's edge.

She ran until she discerned the coming of dawn and then turned around and raced back to her hotel, arriving just as the first rays of light were coloring the morning sky.

When she walked into the lobby, the front-desk clerk lazily picked up his head from the paper he had been reading. An amused smirk appeared on his lips as he examined her.

His guess that she had spent at least part

of the night in someone's bed would have been right.

"Morning," he said with a polite nod of his head, belying the snarky smile on his face that made her want to go rip out his throat.

She refrained from the violence. It was no way to start the day or, in her case, end it.

She skipped the elevator and dashed up the stairs as if she were being pursued, and maybe she was.

Alex remained with her.

She could smell him on her skin. Regretted the warmth of his body fading from hers. Tasted him, she thought, running the tips of her fingers along her lips, where remnants of his kiss lingered.

She was damned, she thought as she hurried into her hotel room, hung the privacy tag on the knob and locked the door.

She didn't want any visitors.

Couldn't imagine facing anyone with the way she was feeling.

Confused. Angry. In love.

Was the last even possible? she wondered.

The last time she had entertained any thoughts of being in love had been nearly two thousand years ago, and look at how badly that had ended. Although there had been that tryst with another vampire last year. But as physically satisfying as that had been, and as entertaining as Blake had been, they had probably known deep in their hearts that love was not meant to be for both of them.

Only…

Blake *had* found love. He had found someone with whom he could spend the rest of his eternal life.

An impossibility for her. Neither love nor forever together had a spot in her destiny.

She pulled off her clothes and dropped them on the floor of the room. They were dry but had that sticky, hard feeling of ocean-wet things.

Dawn was almost done rising outside as she walked toward the bed, feeling the call of the demon to rest. Instead, she walked to the window and moved aside the blackout curtain. Watched as the reds and pinks of the morning sun gave way to another bright blue Miami sky. As those first tentative rays touched her skin, it warmed and then began to sting as the sun rose higher, reminding her of what she was. Of what she would forever be.

Undead and alone.

She couldn't let the night's tryst with Alex make her want things that could never be.

With the sun's sting on her skin, she moved from the window and finally slid beneath the covers.

But as the vampire within dragged her to sleep, she sighed Alex's name and dreamed of him.

The photos from the M.E. were waiting on his desk when he arrived, just minutes after seven in the morning.

Although Alex had gone back to sleep after Stacia had left, it had been a fitful rest as the memories of their first meeting on that long-ago winter night played through his head and mingled with the memories of making love to her.

Fear mixed with loving.

He wondered if that was the only way it could be if you were involved with a vampire.

With a sigh of disgust, he put his cup of

*café con leche* on his desk and tore open the foil wrapping on the toasted Cuban bread he had picked up that morning on the way to work. He took a bite of the buttery bread and flipped open the folder with the photos of both Louie's battered body and that of Ramon Santander, the boyfriend who had been assaulted.

Much as he had hoped, he noticed similar contusions on both of the men, confirming to him that, at a minimum, the same kind of weapon had been used to beat them. Given the M.O., he would put his money on the same people having been behind Santander's assault and Louie's murder.

He bet on the fact that those people were also involved in the disappearance of the women.

Circling the similar bruise patterns on the photos with a Sharpie, he set them aside and took a sip of his coffee. Hot, sweet and strong, it gave him the blast of energy he needed to get going that morning.

It was still too early to call Lieutenant Black, so he turned to the reports from his surveillance team and the tapes from the night before.

Nothing in the report and, unfortunately, zero on the tapes. Yet another night wasted with no clues as to where Andrea or any other of the missing women might be.

As he turned to his computer, he realized that the searches he had been running against the various databases had finally yielded a result—Interpol had an entry for one of his Russian suspects.

Vladimir Pushkin.

Interpol suspected him of at least two murders and listed him as being tied to the Russian mob. His main crimes—drug dealing, assault, murder and prostitution. Interpol had information that Pushkin's prostitution ring was quite large in Russia and had started to spread to other parts of Europe. Pushkin used the money from selling women's favors to buy drugs for his other businesses. Unfortunately, Interpol did not have enough information to charge him with any of the crimes.

Neither did Alex. At least, not yet.

Printing out the search results and Interpol sheet on Pushkin, he made copies for

Black, Brock and Walker, and then tucked one into his file. After, he went through his emails, but there was nothing of use for this case. He printed out the emails relating to his other ongoing investigations, then sat back and considered what to do next about the missing women.

Delgado and Santos, the men he had identified as possible ringleaders in the slavery ring, had yet to make an appearance at the club and it was already Wednesday. He had suspected they would make their move before the weekend. That left only two nights to undergo the transfer of the women, although maybe he had been wrong. Maybe they were willing to take the risk and move the women over the busier weekend nights.

Then there were the Russians, he thought, leaning forward and pulling the photos out of the folder. Reviewing them yet again. The Russians were likely involved in all of the crimes, but there was little evidence to tie them to the misdeeds. Only the word of a witness who had been beaten close to death and might be unreliable on the witness stand because of the brain damage he had suffered.

That was if the man even made it to the trial. If the Russians were tied to the mob, they might make sure that Santander was eliminated before he could testify against them.

The only way to get the Russians behind bars would be to find hard evidence pinning the crimes to them and to do so before their ship pulled out of port next week.

He would have to go over the new information with his team when they had their briefing session later that morning.

As he was closing the file, Orendain came into the room, and from across the width of the space, their gazes connected. Coffee and small brown paper bag in hand, the man sauntered over to Alex's desk.

"Have you got anything yet?" his boss asked.

"Luis Alvarado, one of my informants, was murdered. The M.O. fits that for the beating of one of the missing women's boyfriends."

"Anything else?" Orendain pressed.

"Suspects in the murder and assault are Russian, possibly mob and likely connected to the men we suspect of kidnapping the women," Alex answered, but it was clear that his reply had displeased his boss.

Orendain's lips had thinned into a grim line and he wagged his head back and forth. "Suspect. Possibly connected. Worst of all, what do you have besides a basic murder and assault?"

"I'm sure they're connected to the kidnappings and drug trafficking," Alex urged, but Orendain just kept on shifting his head back and forth.

"Right now you don't have anything that doesn't belong in Miami P.D. jurisdiction. If you don't get more reliable information on the kidnappings and trafficking by Saturday, turn the investigation over to them. I could use you and the others on another case."

"But the women—"

"Are probably dead by now, otherwise they would have made the exchange you thought would happen. Saturday. Case closed."

Without waiting for Alex to reply, Orendain walked away, seemingly at ease with his decision.

Alex could feel no such comfort.

Five missing women, including Andrea McAnn. Five women who would be traded for a shitload of drugs that would end up on Miami streets.

He couldn't fail the women or allow those drugs to be made available for sale. He had to find a way to turn those possibilities and suspicions into concrete facts on which he could base his case.

He had a promise to keep to his friend Dan.

And he always kept his promises.

Her daytime respite was restless, filled with dreams of Cassius and Alex, the two of them mingling together in her mind almost as if to warn her of the danger of believing in love.

Love was just a lure for men to part a woman's thighs and pleasure themselves, her dreams cautioned. A way for men to use women for their own gains, whether sexual or otherwise.

Only, Alex had made no empty promises. Taken nothing and given much, she thought, recalling the pleasure in his arms.

Recalling the way he had made her feel. Realizing then that he had in fact taken something—her heart.

She bolted upright in bed, her body shaking from the emotions roused by her dreams.

Fear about the emotions he had awakened within her.

Concern at the continuing desire to explore those feelings once again.

She rose from the bed and experienced the iciness of air-conditioning on skin warmed by sleep. It chased away the fragile heat that had built beneath the weight of the covers. The false heat, since in her human state her body had no warmth. It was only when the vampire emerged that intense heat flowed through her veins, fueled by a blood feeding.

A blood feeding like the one she needed after her daytime slumber to reanimate her body and get her ready to face another night of life.

Another day in her eternal undead existence.

An existence that she had to live alone, she thought, recalling the warnings in her dreams and remembering what had happened to her the last time she had dared to believe in love.

She went to the refrigerator and removed a blood bag.

Like her body, the blood was cold. Lifeless.

She would find something better later, she thought as she raised the bag to her lips and encountered smooth plastic. She opened her mouth on the bag and released the demon. Sharp fangs exploded and pressed against the plastic, experiencing a moment of resistance.

The resistance reminded her that this was second-rate sustenance.

Human skin provided no such resistance.

Her fangs broke through the plastic of the bag and she drank deeply, draining the blood in just a few short seconds.

Tossing the bag into the garbage, she was heading back to the refrigerator for another feeding when she sensed him nearby.

Alex was here, she thought, walking to the door and laying her hand on it as if by doing so she could touch him.

He knocked.

She didn't answer.

He knocked once again and she sensed his confusion. His anger and concern.

He wanted to know how she was doing after last night. Had wanted to come by this afternoon before he went back to work.

She intended to show him.

She ripped open the door, grabbed his shirt and hauled him into the room.

"Stacia," he said, surprise in his voice at her actions and her appearance.

She stood naked before him, in full vamp mode, and as she released him, he took a step back, obviously alarmed.

"Why are you here?" she asked, the tone of her voice tinged with the rumble of the beast.

"I was…worried."

She laughed and stalked close to him. To his credit, he flinched but didn't move away. "Worried? About me?"

She grabbed hold of his shirtfront once again and lifted him a few inches off the ground. "Look at me. Look at what I am. Do you think I need your concern?"

For good measure, she tossed him away. He went flying across the room and landed in a sprawling heap, but he quickly came to his feet, his hands outstretched.

"Why are you doing this?" he asked, taking a step toward her.

She held up her hand and invoked her elder power, stopping him in his tracks. "Why? You know why, Alex. You feel the same way as I do. Admit it."

The push of her power kept him away. Alex could feel her restraining him almost as if she had her hands on his body. And he couldn't deny what she had said.

Although she was naked in all her stunning female glory, his gaze was affixed to her face. Her inhuman vampire face with its bloodstained fangs and weird blue-green gaze, which seemed to be glowing brighter than he had ever seen it.

Fear took hold in his gut. Fear of what she was and what she could do, only…

"I feel it, Stacia. And yes, I'm afraid of what you are. But you're also afraid of what I am."

She took a step toward him and chuckled. "Afraid of what you are? You're a puny human. If I wanted to, I could kill you with just a thought."

As if to prove her point, his throat closed up, cutting off his breath.

"Stacia, love," he managed to say in a strangled hiss.

"Love," she snarled, obviously annoyed, but released him from her control. "This isn't love, Alex. It's lust and sex. Nothing more."

*Nothing more,* he thought, and maybe she was right. Maybe the wisest thing would be to leave it at that.

To leave her and forget all that had happened between them.

To drive from his mind and heart the possibility that it was more. That it was love.

"You're right, Stacia. We both know it's nothing more."

The tone of his voice was injured but filled with resignation.

In the space of a human heartbeat, he was moving toward the door, where he hesitated for only a moment.

"Goodbye," he said and left.

The thud of the door closing reverberated through her body. And although he had walked out the door, she knew he remained on the other side of the wood. Hesitant about leaving her in this fashion, while sure that the wisest thing to do was to leave.

She also sensed many of the same emotions that had troubled him when he had first arrived at her door still haunting him. Concern and anger.

Longing.

Despite all that had just transpired, all that he had seen of her, he still had feelings for her.

Much as she couldn't deny that she still had feelings for him.

Despite the caution in her dreams and all that she had learned over the millennia, she needed what he had shown her.

She needed to believe that love was possible, because if it wasn't, what was the sense in having eternal life?

She lingered by the door as did he, torn by the desire to open it and show him her love as well as her desire to protect herself from the heartache she was sure would follow.

As time passed, she sensed his departure,

and for one crazy moment, she considered chasing after him, but restrained herself.

She was a vampire elder. Going after him would be the equivalent of royalty chasing after a commoner.

Such pairings never ended well, she reminded herself and pulled away from the door. She needed to get dressed and ready to find dinner that night. Maybe even search for someone to share her bed and drive thoughts of Alex from her mind.

But as she prepared, each and every action brought a reminder of all they had shared. And as she exited the hotel and her vamp senses picked up the trace of his scent, Stacia acknowledged just how hard it was going to be to drive him out of her heart.

## Chapter 17

Only two days left to go, Alex thought later that night, running his fingers along the marble surface of the bar. The stone was cold and smooth, reminding him of Stacia's dead skin. Warning him that Louie had ended up in the morgue because Alex had involved him in this case.

A case that was going nowhere fast, much like his relationship with Stacia was stuck in an untenable state.

As had happened the past few nights, there had been no sign of his suspects, Delgado or Santos, at the Widget. The Russians hadn't been back, either, maybe lying low because they knew someone was asking questions about them. Or maybe because they had the women and were preparing to leave with them.

Black had warned him to watch his back in case Louie had blown his cover during his beating, but so far, Alex had no indication that anyone was after him—other than Stacia.

In a way he wished Delgado and his friends would try something to take him down since at least he might make some progress on the case if they did.

And it suddenly occurred to him that maybe he had been mistaken all along in waiting for the suspects to show up at the Widget to meet a woman to grab. Although that had been the case for Andrea and most of the other women, all of the women had also been to a number of other clubs as well as the Widget on the night they had been taken.

He pulled out his cell phone, dialed his team and advised them that he was taking a break to go check something out.

Quickly he went to his convertible, yanked his laptop from underneath the passenger-side seat and, using his broadband card, connected to his office computer. He opened up his electronic files, reviewing the various witness accounts of the women's activities on the nights of their disappearances and then his notes and lists. As he examined all of the paperwork, one name popped up at him again and again—Vida Loca.

Each of the women had been at that bar also on the night she had disappeared. In fact, every one of them had been there immediately before heading to the Widget.

Was that where either Delgado or Santos selected the women for later kidnapping? Had they decided to grab them before they ever even made it to the other club?

He shut down the laptop and called his team.

Walker answered the phone. "What's up, boss?"

"I've got a hunch. All of the women were at the same club immediately before heading to the Widget."

"You think that's where they might have

been bagged?" Walker asked, and in the background he heard Brock say, "Or tagged."

"Bagged and/or tagged is possible. I'm heading over there for a little bit. I'll keep you posted," he said and hung up.

Since Vida Loca was only a few blocks away and all of the witness testimonies indicated that the women had walked from one location to the next, he did the same. He strode briskly down Lincoln Road toward Collins where he turned, moved past the Loews Hotel and then to Ocean Drive. With each step he kept vigilant for any signs of activity.

For a possible glimpse of Stacia as she sought out her next meal. Despite everything that had happened that day, thoughts of her still lingered in his mind.

Vida Loca was at the northernmost edge of Ocean Drive, close to the Tides hotel. Much smaller than the Widget, it would provide a hunter a better locale for bagging or tagging prey.

Despite its smaller size, a decent crowd waited to get into the club. He knew the bouncer well, and as he approached, the man gave a curt nod of his head and permitted him to enter.

The club was much busier than it had been the night he had met Louie there. Filled with locals, students on college break and an assortment of American and European tourists, there was a nice selection of attractive women in a concentrated space.

Like shooting fish in a barrel, he thought, and wondered why he hadn't realized it before.

He weaved through the crowd, examining the bar's patrons. Imagining what he might do if he were one of the suspects—or maybe even his undead lover. Picking out potential targets as he strolled past the throng of people on the dance floor and the tables lining the walls of the club. The music was loud tonight, a fusion of Latin and hip-hop beats that had the crowd moving animatedly to the music.

He was nearing the long, illuminated bar when he sensed her power.

Stacia, he thought, vainly trying to ignore the way his heart sped up and desire rose in him at the prospect of seeing her again.

Sure enough, she was at the end of the bar, speaking to a man. Probably sizing him up to be her dinner, he thought, dragging his sight from them only to find Omar Santos sitting at the opposite end of the bar. He was chatting with a man who had his back to Alex. The discussion seemed heated based on Santos's gesticulations.

Alex slipped into the crowd on the dance floor and approached from that direction, using the people around him to hide his presence until he was close enough to identify the other man—Delgado—and listen in on the conversation.

It was hard due to the loud music and the shift of the crowd, which kept moving to and fro like the ebb of the tide, allowing him to only catch snippets of the discussion.

"One more...*estas loco,*" Santos said.

Delgado's back was to him, making his response an unintelligible murmur.

"No...too dangerous," Santos replied in Spanish.

The sharp slap of a hand on the wooden bar counter registered and then he caught movement from the corner of his eye—Delgado leaving Santos behind. Clearly Delgado was in charge and calling the shots, no matter how upset his partner appeared to be.

Alex drifted away, trying to follow Delgado to see where he went in the club. He hoped he would head somewhere private in the space, but Delgado just continued right out the front door.

And maybe straight to the Widget.

He was far enough away from Santos that he could dial his team without being observed, and he did, warning them to keep an eye out for Delgado.

Then he returned to his surveillance of Santos, managing to snare an empty seat halfway between Stacia at one end and Santos at the other. Santos had not moved from his spot at the bar. As Alex watched him, Santos downed another drink, clearly unhappy with whatever Delgado had commanded.

A few minutes later, Alex's cell phone vibrated twice, signaling that he had a text message. He took a quick look. It was a message from his team advising that Delgado had just entered the Widget.

Bingo, Alex thought. Something they could arguably call progress.

Alex mentally repeated Santos's earlier words to Delgado, reaching only one assumption—Delgado wanted Santos to grab another woman. And if that assumption was correct, it meant that the men might be getting ready to transfer their shipment of human contraband, likely to the Russians whose ship was due to leave port next week.

He remained at the bar, watching Santos. Waiting for him to make a move, only Santos just kept downing drinks, seemingly determined to ignore the command he had been given.

Alex was sitting there when he noticed the man next to him moving away, but he also sensed something else—the familiar force of Stacia's power taking control of the man.

She eased into the space beside him, but he fought the desire to look at her, keeping his gaze on Santos, although he said, "What are you doing here?"

From the corner of his eye, he saw her shrug. "I wish I knew. What are you doing here?"

Alex barely moved, but it was enough for Stacia to determine that his interest was directed toward the end of the bar.

From behind the protection of Alex's body, she examined those at the end of the long, illuminated counter, determined to discover what interested him more than she did. She reached out to those seated at the end of the bar with her elder power and sensed the anger of the man farthest away. Experienced the blackness within him, a soul-deep darkness as evil as that of some of the undead she had met over her long existence.

"It's him, isn't it?" she whispered to Alex, who finally deigned to look her way. The movement brought him close, his lips barely an inch from her face.

"Him? Who?" he asked, his gaze searching her features. Conflict alive in the depths of his eyes.

"The handsome one at the end," she answered, although the stranger was nowhere near as good-looking as Alex.

A puzzled look flickered across her lover's face. "How do you know that?"

"You don't live as long as I have without

being able to sense danger," she admitted and motioned for the bartender, aware that Alex was at work and their conversation had to seem normal so that his cover wouldn't be blown.

"Mojito," she said, and when the bartender delivered the drink a couple of minutes later, Alex tossed out a bill to pay for the drink.

"Thank you," she said, but Alex quickly retorted, "Don't thank me. We both know—"

"I'm not here to cause problems." She picked up the mojito and took a bracing gulp of the drink, although there was nothing about the alcohol that would give her Dutch courage.

"What are you here to do, then?" he asked bluntly, his gaze locking on hers like a heat-seeking missile zeroing in on a target.

She honestly didn't know why she was there, given their exchange earlier that afternoon. But something had driven her out into the night—driven her to find him, she had to admit. Now that she was beside him, it was difficult to deny that he was like catnip to her system—attractive and intoxicating. It was also difficult to ignore that he was angry since she was interfering with his investigation once again.

The honor and duty he put above all—even those he loved.

But he didn't love her. He did not want to care for her.

And because he could not fail because women might end up in slavery, he would not give her his attention.

Likewise, because she knew what it was like to lose not only her life to a man, but also her freedom, it suddenly came to her what she had to do to make things right.

"I want to help you."

Shock blossomed on his face. "Help? You think you can help?"

"What do you want? I can control him. Have him lead us—"

Alex covered her mouth with his hand. "I can't rely on what you can do."

She eased her hand over his, remembering how much pleasure he had brought her with that hand. Recalling the tenderness as he had touched her with it. She cradled his hand in hers and reluctantly brought it to the surface of the bar. She would have much rather had him touch her again.

"Why not?" she asked.

"Because I need to act legally. Otherwise, I'm no better than they are."

As a vampire, her existence had become one of the ends justifying the means. You took what you needed without a thought to the consequences of it. Restraint such as his was something hard to comprehend. Even more difficult to follow.

"If it were someone you loved, would you be so honorable?" she challenged.

She was sorry she asked as intense sorrow filled his features and his words confirmed the reason for his pain. "You were there that night. You dare to ask if I'd give up a loved one in exchange for what duty demands?"

He had sat there watching his beloved Diana struggling for life, but she knew that if he could have completed the mission that night he would have. No, she was certain he wouldn't sacrifice duty for love. And because of that, she understood he wouldn't break his demanding code of honor for the passion they had shared.

Ardor might have called them together,

but it wasn't a strong enough bond to survive even the smallest of challenges.

"I'm sorry—"

"We seem to be saying that a lot to each other these last few days. Why is that, do you think?" The tone of his voice was calmer now and tinged with regret.

Regret for what had been or remorse for what would not happen between them? she wondered briefly before she said, "Maybe because we're both passionate about what we do. What we want."

"What is it that you want, Stacia?" he asked, twining his fingers with hers and exerting gentle pressure as if to urge her to be truthful.

But the truth—that she cared for him more than she ever had anything else—would only complicate things, she realized. Instead she said, "I want to survive. I want to live another two thousand years."

She didn't add that she didn't want the next two thousand years to be alone. That would be disclosing too much.

With a nod, he said, "I wish I could understand such selfish want, but I can't. Maybe that's why we're always at odds."

His words cut deep. More than she could admit, but she controlled herself and gracefully withdrew from him.

Alex watched her retreat physically. Felt the loss of her touch and the withdrawal of his connection with her.

"Stacia?" he questioned, sorry for his harsh words but unable to take them back. He couldn't understand a creature such as she was. One who survived by taking to fulfill their own needs regardless of how they hurt others. One who offered nothing to anyone else because of the demands of their own self-centered existence.

But even as those thoughts crossed his mind, the little voice in his head chastised him, reminding him of how much she had given him in the past few days. How much pleasure and satisfaction that went beyond the physical. She had brought a light into his life that he hadn't experienced in too long.

He cared for her despite it all, but held back any gentle words for her. He needed the distance between them.

She offered him a sad smile, leaned forward and brushed a kiss across his lips. In whispered tones, she said, "This is something else we seem to always be saying—goodbye, Alex."

Before he could register a protest, she was gone, her vamp speed making her invisible as she left him.

Grief filled him, but as he had told her earlier, he couldn't allow his emotions to cloud what he had to do. To interfere with his duties and responsibilities.

And so he turned back to the bar and to where Santos still sat at the end of the counter, finishing yet another drink. Alex was about to order himself a drink, but Stacia's mojito sat there, nearly finished. The mark of her lipstick along the rim of the glass.

No sense wasting it, he thought, and took hold of the glass. Ran his fingers through the sweat on the outside of it. Inched upward to lightly pass his thumb across the imprint of her lipstick, smearing it off. Wiping at it until all remains of it were gone, only...

It wouldn't be that easy to remove the mark she had made on his soul, he realized. He forced that thought away with a big gulp of the drink and concentrated on Santos, waiting for him to make his move.

## Chapter 18

Something was different, Andrea thought.

There were new voices out in the hallway.

Sounds of activity.

She rose from her corner and cautiously inched toward the door. Placed her ear against the wood and listened.

Multiple footsteps sounded beyond, along with the murmur of voices. There must be several men there, she thought, hearing the different pitches and accents as well as footsteps growing louder as they neared her room. Shadows danced along the large gap at the bottom of the door, marking their passage down the hall.

"The thin man says we move soon," one man said, his voice fairly clear as if he was right by her door. He had a thick accent. Not Spanish like that of the one hooded man who brought in her food. This accent was harsher, like German.

"*Da,* soon" was the reply, a little more muted, and Andrea realized it wasn't a German accent, but Russian.

Russians? she wondered and pressed her ear tighter to the wood, but the men had drifted away, making it impossible for her to make out any other parts of the conversation.

Still she waited by the door, hopeful that she might hear something else. Anything that might explain why she had been taken and what they planned to do with her.

No other sounds came, and she finally returned to her corner, sat down and huddled there. They had fed her many hours earlier so her hunger was at bay for the moment. It also meant that it must be nighttime. Possibly late at night, since she had fallen asleep but awakened when she heard the noises in the hallway.

Of course, she slept a lot lately.

What else was there to do when you were locked in a room not much bigger than a closet with nothing to do and only the dim light from a dollar-store night-light for illumination?

*You can pray,* she thought.

She had been doing a lot of that lately, hoping that someone might answer her prayers and set her free. Wishing that her dad was searching for her and would come to rescue her.

She hadn't appreciated what her dad had done as a DEA agent. She had been too busy rebelling and messing up her life. It was only later, when her troubles had ruined their lives, that she had come to see who he really was.

The past few years, with him by her side, she had finally gotten her life under control. She had finally seen his strength and realized he was a hero. The kind of hero who did what was right without expecting to be on the front page of the daily newspaper.

Andrea didn't think that she had ever told him that—that he was a hero. She had always been jealous of all the time he spent away from his family, never understanding that he did it so they would all be safe. So that other people would be safe.

Sadly, she understood it now.

She only hoped that she would be able to return home so she could finally tell her father how she felt. So that she could continue down the path on which she had started and become a better person.

Andrea closed her eyes, not to sleep, but to pray some more.

*Please Lord, let me go home. Let us all go home,* she thought, thinking of the other female voices she had heard off and on during the course of her imprisonment.

Hoping they had heroes waiting for them, as well.

Alex smiled with pleasure at the still shots taken from the videotapes his team had been able to record the night before. Not only were there pictures of Delgado heading into the Widget via a back door, but they had also managed to get video of him leaving with two of the Russians.

Not Pushkin, unfortunately.

There had also been no transfer of money or any other obvious signs that a deal was going down that night. The men had been relatively subdued and had said nothing of consequence to one another while they were within surveillance range.

But together with Delgado's conversation with Santos at Vida Loca, Alex was convinced that they would shortly be exchanging some of the missing women for the drugs Louie had mentioned.

Armed with that information, he prepared a report for his boss, printed it out and took it to Orendain, eager to share the progress they had made.

Orendain was in his office, but he was on the phone. As he noticed Alex's approach, he swiveled his leather executive chair around, presenting his back to Alex.

So his boss had returned to that, Alex thought, recalling the many times in the past when Orendain had dismissed him. But with the freedom of Dan's daughter and the other women at stake, he maintained his cool and waited patiently.

Nearly fifteen minutes later, Orendain

hung up the phone and circled back around slowly. His face hardened with annoyance as he realized Alex had not left after the earlier snub.

"This better be important, Garcia." Orendain picked up a stack of pink message slips and began shuffling through them as Alex walked up to stand before his desk.

"We've got some solid progress on the case," he said, but Orendain didn't lift his head.

Alex wanted to drop his report smack on those annoying pieces of pink but instead he calmly placed the report before his boss. "We've finally made a link between Delgado, Santos and the Russians. We think the transfer of the women will happen shortly."

His boss tossed aside his messages and picked up the report. Leaning back in his chair, Orendain thumbed through it slowly, almost painfully so, and then disdainfully flipped it back in Alex's direction. "You've made what kind of connection, Garcia? You still don't have proof of any kidnapping or drug dealing. All you still have is basic assault and murder cases."

Alex couldn't believe what he was hearing. "You can't be serious. We've got possible—"

"I'm going to recommend that this case be transferred to Miami P.D. Unless you have something else by Saturday—"

Alex splayed his hands on Orendain's desk, using his greater height to lean forward until he was nearly nose-to-nose with the other man. "You would risk losing these women because of some political bullshit or petty beef with me?"

Orendain laughed uneasily and pushed away from his desk and Alex. "If you think this is politics or some beef, go over my head and see what happens. They'll tell you the same thing—there's nothing in this report that's in our jurisdiction."

Alex hated that Orendain was right about the current state of the investigation and being a hard-ass about it. If Alex had just another few days, he would get the link they needed to keep the investigation with DEA.

Orendain was not about to give him those few days. But Alex also was not about to let it go so easily.

"When we find these women—emphasis

on the *when*—I'm going to make sure that every news source in town knows about your little game and how close we came to losing them because of your ego."

He spun around and stalked out of the room, his anger barely leashed. His fists clenched at his sides, resisting the urge to punch the wall. Although for a moment, until sanity returned, he did consider going back and smashing Orendain.

At his desk, he printed out an updated report for his team, including Orendain's instructions and deadline so that all would be clear about what was at stake.

When the team assembled later that morning in one of the briefing rooms, he provided them with the news.

"Orendain can't be serious," Walker said as she finished reading the report Alex had created.

"He's a horse's ass," Brock commented and tossed the papers onto the top of the table in the briefing room.

"For once we actually agree on something," Walker added and copied his actions, flipping her report onto the tabletop.

"I hate to admit it, but he's right about what we've got right now," Alex said, playing devil's advocate.

"*Right now* being the key words. In another few days, we might have enough to connect everything and break this case wide-open." Brock emphasized it by broadly spreading his outstretched hands.

"And save five innocent women," Walker added softly, clearly dismayed that other women might suffer because of Orendain's stupidity and ego.

While Alex agreed, it was his role to keep his team in order and their attention centered on the case.

"Okay, so let's go over what we've got and how we can make something happen with it," he said.

The three started reviewing all their available evidence, and by the time they disbanded to deal with their assorted tasks, Alex was hopeful they would soon make a break in the case. Because of that, he calmed down from his earlier anger with Orendain. Despite that forced composure, he was more determined than ever to recover the women and prove Orendain wrong.

At the meeting he had split the team, assigning Brock to keep an eye on Vida Loca while Walker stayed at the Widget. He would make visits to both locations to see if Santos would follow Delgado's orders and lure another woman to her imprisonment.

In the meantime, he had some legwork on a couple of other cases and needed to follow up with the medical examiner to see if any of the forensic evidence on Louie's murder linked back to the Russians. Luckily for him, his call to the morgue revealed that the medical examiner had run some detailed analyses of the bruise patterns, which confirmed the same type of weapon had been used both in the assault on Ramon Santander and in Louie's murder. Not only that, they had been able to determine that the most likely weapon had been a large monkey wrench—the kind used in boiler rooms on ships like the Russians'.

"Thanks for that," he said to the M.E.

"If you can get me the wrench, we might be able to make a match to the contusions on the body. Maybe even be lucky enough to find blood and tissue remnants."

"I'll try," he promised, concerned that even though they had connected the two crimes, he still did not have enough probable cause to get a warrant to search the Russians' ship.

Frustrated, he hung up, determined to make something happen before Orendain's artificial deadline arrived.

## Chapter 19

Her internal vampire alarm clock woke Stacia from her daytime rest.

She stretched in bed, driving the lethargy from her limbs. Charged with a sense of determination she had not experienced in centuries.

Tonight she had something to do besides finding dinner, although she would deal with that first so that she could be at full strength for what she intended.

And because of what she planned to do, she had to look especially desirable tonight.

With a definite outcome in mind, she

prepared a bath, perfuming the water with jasmine-scented bath oil the hotel had provided. Making sure the water was as hot as she could bear to drive away the chill of her human state.

As she waited for the bath to fill, she poured herself some blood from her stash and slowly sipped it. Trailing a finger through the water, she considered what a shame it was to not have someone with whom to share the luxury of the large tub. Quite a change from her earlier aversion to sharing a bath.

Unfortunately, the only someone with whom she wished to share her tub was decidedly off-limits. Alex presented too many complications in her life, much as she did in his.

They were both better off alone.

Or at least away from each other until things were more settled. If there was such a thing as settled in Alex's life.

As he had warned her, and as she had realized from his last assignment, Alex put his work and duty before anything else in his life.

Even before love, assuming that they could

call the warped emotion both pulling them together and yanking them apart love.

Giving him a break from his duty was one of the reasons she had decided on her course of action for tonight. She hoped to hasten the completion of his assignment, but not just for her own selfish reasons.

Despite Alex's belief that in her immortal state she cared only for herself, the other reason she had decided to act was to make sure that the women who had been kidnapped did not end up as slaves.

She also had firsthand experience of such an existence and would not abide that happening to any other woman if she could help it.

With those goals in mind, she finished the first glass of blood and then refilled it just before she slipped into the aromatic warmth of the bath.

The caress of the water was heady, surrounding her with its embrace but falling far short of the pleasure of a lover's arms. Later that night, if she were unable to complete what she planned, she would find someone to fulfill her. To give her pleasure.

She banished the annoying voice in her head that said she would be hard-pressed to find anyone who had satisfied her the way Alex had. But Alex would have to wait for now.

When the water grew chilled and her glass of blood had been drained long ago, she eased from the tub and dried herself. Carefully dressed in a confection sure to arouse interest.

The black undergarment of the dress hugged every ample curve of her body while the loose, diaphanous shift that fitted over it fluttered and danced as she walked, playing an enticing game of peekaboo.

Perfect, she thought, whirling before the mirror, imagining how she might appear to others.

She slicked her hair back from her face, aware that the perfection of her features would likewise beguile. With some shadow to highlight the exotic tilt of her eyes and bloodred lipstick, she had no doubt she would be able to reel in her prey.

And if her basic physical allure failed, there was always her vamp power to assist.

Alex might be honorable, but she had no such qualms.

She knew what she wanted to accomplish and would do so by whatever means necessary. No woman should have to suffer as she had so long ago.

She should not have to suffer the pangs of denial as she waited for Alex.

With that determination firmly cemented in her psyche, she exited her room and sped into the night.

Alex maneuvered through the crowd, vigilant for any of their suspects or signs of atypical happenings. Stopping to dance with one woman he knew in order to keep his cover. Afterward, he took her to the bar for a drink, made some polite talk, but then his cell phone vibrated, alerting him that he had a message.

"Excuse me," he said to the woman and quickly read the missive from Brock.

Santos just entered Vida Loca.

"Something important?" the woman said and leaned toward him, as if to read the note, but he snapped it shut before she had a chance.

"I have a deal going down. You know how it is," he replied, trying to maintain his cover. The woman, like so many others on the strip, believed that he was involved in the local drug trade.

"If it's anything good, let me know. I could use a little pick-me-up." She reached into her purse, pulled out a hundred and slipped it across the surface of the bar to him.

Alex smiled and paternally patted her hand. "This shit isn't for you, *amorcito*. You deserve better," he said and motioned to the bartender.

When he came over, he handed the bartender several bills. "A bottle of Cristal for my lady."

Before she could protest, he dropped a quick kiss on her cheek and hurried from the bar, intent on finding out what Santos was up to at the other location.

Outside on the street, he examined the line of people waiting to enter the Widget. Among them were several gorgeous young women, and he worried that one of them might be taken tonight to fulfill the instructions he had overheard the night before.

But if Santos was at the other club, maybe that would be his hunting ground tonight, Alex thought as he began the walk toward Collins. As he hurried to the other club, he flipped open the phone and dialed Brock. The agent answered immediately, but Alex had to strain to hear him above the background noise from the crowd and music.

"What do you have for me?" he asked.

"Our friend entered about five minutes ago. I followed him inside. He's been walking around since then, glad-handing some old friends. No other action yet."

"Okay. Keep an eye on him. If he approaches a woman, make sure you stay close enough to track him, but do not engage. We need to know where he takes her."

"Roger," Brock replied and hung up.

Alex quickened his pace, determined to reach the bar and assist with the surveillance. It took him only a few more minutes to arrive at Vida Loca. With a nod to the bouncer, he skipped past the line of people and into the establishment. As at the Widget, there was quite a selection of nubile women parading around.

Inside, he immediately caught sight of Santos at the bar. He appeared to be alone at first, but then Santos leaned to the left, clearly engaged in a conversation with some-one.

Maybe even some unlucky woman, he thought.

But then the crowd parted before him and he realized Stacia was sitting beside his sus-pect. She was smiling flirtatiously and San-tos was totally eating it up.

Of course, what man, undead or alive, could resist that kind of temptation?

He couldn't really describe what she was wearing. Suffice it to say that every time she moved, the fabric seemed to caress her body and offer revealing glimpses of her volup-tuous form beneath the see-through fabric. Her hair was slicked back from her face, dis-playing her high, sculpted cheekbones and tantalizing cocoa-brown eyes that had been artfully highlighted with eye shadow. As she smiled, her human teeth perfectly white and straight, his body reacted, reminding him of the pleasure he had found in her arms.

He sucked in a breath and drove away both desire and anger since she was well aware of who Santos was and had clearly chosen to interfere in his investigation.

Keeping Santos and Stacia in his line of sight, he strolled through the club until he encountered Brock. The agent was leaning against a wall close to Santos, a glass in his hand, looking just like any of a number of the other men in the establishment.

Alex paused at the bar to order a seltzer with mint and lime, then approached Brock. He stood beside the agent, took a sip of the seltzer and asked beneath his breath, "When did the woman with Santos arrive?"

The agent shook his head, befuddled. "One moment she was on the dance floor and then Santos caught sight of her. He left the bar and went straight up to her, almost like he knew her. Then he invited her to join him."

Did she use her vampire powers? Alex wondered, but then again, even without her undead ability, Stacia could likely attract any man she wanted. And he could say with a clear conscience that he hadn't instructed her to use her vampire powers on Santos. She didn't really have to, he thought.

Even now, as he watched over her as she engaged their suspect, the pull of her beauty and sexiness was undeniable. He stood there fascinated by her actions. Seduced by the way she smiled and leaned toward Santos, enticing him closer. Ensnaring him with her feminine wiles. A girlie little laugh. A fleeting caress of her hand along the side of his face.

Some time passed and it was clear Santos was not going to rush off anywhere with Stacia. Alex whispered to Brock as he kept the vigil beside him, "I'll stay and keep an eye on these two. Why don't you head outside and watch the perimeter? See if there's anything else going on."

With an abrupt nod, Brock departed, leaving Alex to monitor Santos and worry about what Stacia planned to do.

Men were so easy, Stacia thought, casting a knowing smile at the man beside her as he preened, dropping hints about his connections and how he could make her night special.

It hadn't taken her much to catch his attention. Just a little dance a few feet away. She hadn't even used a scintilla of her vampire power to get him to come over.

She had been hoping for a little more difficulty to the hunt to eat up some time. Now she was stuck here with him, listening to him crow like a rooster. Counting the interminable minutes until he decided to make some other move, preferably one that would take her to where he had the missing women Alex was so eager to locate.

Women she would spare from a fate such as she had suffered.

"Is something wrong?" Santos asked, and she realized she must have allowed either anger or inattention to become apparent.

Forcing a sexy smile to her lips, she said, "It's just a little noisy in here."

Santos nodded and glanced around the room. "Kind of crowded, as well."

She tracked his gaze, and as she did so, she caught sight of Alex by the side of the room.

He nodded as her gaze collided with his, and she allowed her vamp power to reach out to him. As she did so, she detected his annoyance, but also his concern.

With a soft push of power, she implanted her thoughts in his head.

*Don't worry. I know what I'm doing.*

Stacia returned her interest to the man beside her, who raised his hand and ordered them another round of drinks. She supposed some might have found him attractive. His features were refined, and the clothes he wore were expensive and stylish. They made him appear elegant, but that illusion was shattered the moment he opened his mouth. He was clearly a man off the streets who lacked any real refinement.

That was further evidenced as he spent the next hour regaling her with stories of the many celebrities he had met and could supposedly call friends. With each name that he dropped, she oohed and aahed appropriately, knowing what he needed to hear. Stroking his substantial ego.

She was certain of what she had to do to accomplish her goal—make this man want to take her somewhere to prove his supposed reputation.

When he asked her to danc, she acquiesced, moving her body to the heavy bass beats of the music. Teasing him with glimpses of her curves in the tight-fitting undergarment. Brushing against him occasionally until he finally grabbed hold of her waist and yanked her close, issuing a warning as he did so.

"*Niña,* you're playing with fire."

She chuckled coquettishly and whispered against the shell of his ear, "I'm not afraid of a little heat."

He groaned at her words and wrapped his arm around her waist, holding her near as he dry humped her in time to the music. His erection, smallish and thin, was like a pencil jabbing at her midsection, but she endured it. Encouraged him with the subtler shift of her hips until he was trembling beside her.

"*Amorcito,* let's go somewhere more private," he said.

*Bingo,* she thought.

## Chapter 20

Alex endured the spectacle, telling himself that the sight of another man close to having sex with Stacia on the dance floor shouldn't bother him.

But it did. A lot.

It took all his control to rein in his personal feelings. Anger at her interference. Fear at what might happen to her. Jealousy as the other man touched her.

He suffered through the show, knowing that any interference on his part would blow his cover and possibly bring an end to the assignment.

The assignment that had to take priority over all that he was feeling. Over anything personal because of the lives of the missing women.

Sipping on the room-temperature dregs of his drink, he patiently waited for something to happen. If Santos did in fact need to kidnap one more woman, Stacia had certainly made herself the prime candidate.

As the song ended and the DJ announced that he was being replaced by someone else, Santos suddenly pulled away from Stacia. He had a firm grip on her arm, however, as he led her away from the dance floor and in the direction of the door. As Stacia followed Santos, she took a moment to glance in Alex's direction and send him another vamp-powered communication.

*We're going somewhere more private.*

He grabbed his cell phone, all the while thinking about how freaky it was that he heard her voice in his head as if she was speaking directly to him. Since Brock was monitoring the exterior of Vida Loca, Alex texted him that their suspects were on the move and that he should hang back for a moment to see if anything happened after their departure. Then he strode toward the exit, intent on following Stacia and Santos at a discreet distance.

Luckily, it was a nice night and there were still enough people out on the street that he didn't stick out as he tracked them. He assumed they would be headed to the Widget, and his assumption wasn't wrong. He called ahead to warn Walker of their imminent arrival, and in less than ten minutes, they were at the door to the other club.

The bouncer immediately allowed Santos and Stacia to enter.

Alex hung back, attempting to make his pursuit less obvious. When a few minutes had passed, he strolled past the bouncer without incident and entered the establishment.

Inside it took him several minutes to locate his suspects due to the size of the space and the crowded conditions.

He finally found Santos and Stacia seated at the bar, heads bent close together.

The waiter placed mojitos in front of them and they merrily made a toast. Stacia downed her glass with a few quick gulps, and Santos immediately signaled the waiter to bring another.

As he had before, Alex took a spot several feet away so he could observe and make his move when the time was right.

Stacia guessed at what Santos was hoping for—that she get blind drunk so he would be able to take control. Make her do what he wanted with her.

With that knowledge, she chugged down one mojito and was on her way to finishing the next when she tasted something off. The second drink had a bitterness to it that had nothing to do with an inexpert mixing of the lime and mint.

Could it be a drug? she wondered, not that it would make a difference to her undead metabolism. Vampires didn't react to drugs the way humans did.

As she met Santos's gaze, she detected slyness there. His interest now had nothing to do with his earlier bump and grind and everything to do with the fact that he thought she would soon be indisposed. That he would have power over her.

Because of that, she feigned upset and said, "I'm feeling a little dizzy."

Neither surprise nor concern crossed over his face, a testament to his awareness that a drug had been in the drink. "Would you like to go lie down?"

"I think so," she said and rose from the stool, but mimicked dizziness by grabbing hold of his shoulder to steady herself.

"I'll help you," he said and eased his arm around her waist.

He guided her toward the entrance to the private rooms, and as he did so, she once again noticed Alex by the side of the club. He was on the balls of his feet, ready to come rushing to her aid. Surprising her because he was placing his worry for her over the assignment.

She couldn't let him compromise what he had to do for her.

This time she used more than her vampire thoughts to prevent him from doing so. She sent a blast of energy in his direction, freezing him to the spot as she said, *Don't stop me. I want to find the other women.*

*Don't do this,* she heard back, which surprised her. Normally only other vamps could reply mentally, but she didn't have time to consider the reasons for such an intimate connection with him.

She needed to perfect her act so that Santos would take her into the private areas and maybe put her together with the missing women.

He guided her past the bouncer to the exclusive rooms and she really played it up, tripping over her feet and leaning on him heavily. When they entered the restricted area, the door locked behind them with a solid thunk, the sound troubling.

Santos looked at her, seemingly puzzled. Was she playing her dizziness up too much or not enough? she wondered. Just then, she caught a glimpse of another man approaching.

"Why isn't she out already?" the man chastised, obviously perturbed by the fact she was still awake.

Rather than risk a problem, she closed her eyes and went limp in Santos's arms. Not expecting the sudden collapse, Santos nearly dropped her, which earned a complaint from the other man.

"Don't bruise the merchandise. Put her in number five. We'll be rounding them all up in there within the hour."

All of them. Within the hour, she thought and broadcast that information back to Alex, only this time, she wasn't sure that he got her message. He might be too far away and behind the thickness of that solid-sounding door.

A niggle of apprehension, just a niggle, passed through her that the cavalry might not be able to rush in to save them.

But it was just a little concern since, after all, she was a vampire elder with immense power. She had no doubt she could handle a few humans.

As Santos carried her along what seemed to be a hall, she reached out and sensed others, but she assumed that was expected since patrons also frequented this area. Santos continued moving along, and as he did so, the area around them grew quieter. Then he began walking down stairs, his strength clearly taxed by the dead weight of her in his arms.

The air grew cooler and became tinged with a thick, musty scent. At the foot of the stairs, Santos moved forward, and this time, she detected some people along the hall. Just a few, maybe three or four. Women, she could tell from the push of their life forces.

Santos finally stopped, fumbling with a doorknob for a second before he entered and let her slip to the ground. Stacia lay there quietly, waiting for him to leave and the door to close behind him before opening her eyes.

The room was small. Barely more than a closet. It had a rank smell—a mix of human sweat and excrement. Someone had been kept here for some time. Another woman possibly, she thought since mixed in with the unpleasant odors was the lingering scent of an expensive perfume.

From beyond the door came the sounds of a struggle followed by a slap and a woman's cry of pain.

The door opened and she feigned sleep once more.

"Get in there," Santos commanded and tossed in another woman.

After the door closed, Stacia opened her eyes and met the frightened gaze of the new occupant. Barely a woman. She couldn't be more than about twenty-two, if that. She was attractive with long blond hair and a voluptuous body. And she was tall—she had nearly a foot on Stacia's petite height as Stacia came to her feet.

The young woman glanced at Stacia, confusion on her face.

Stacia walked to stand before her, experiencing unexpected commiseration with the woman. She surprised herself by offering her hand, and as the other woman took it, she said, "I'm here to help."

Alex cursed beneath his breath as he continued to wait close to the entrance of the private area. It had been nearly twenty minutes since Stacia had disappeared with Santos into that section. He had advised his team to be on the lookout for signs of any activity, but so far there had been nothing.

How long could he wait for them to emerge?

What if they didn't? What if Stacia had just become the next missing woman?

An icy chill took hold of his gut as he considered that possibility, but then reason resumed rule.

Stacia was an immortal. A powerful and undead immortal who could take care of herself. Hadn't she told him that more times than he could count?

But as more and more time elapsed, deep worry set in and he cursed beneath his breath, feeling impotent.

He couldn't just stand there anymore. Problem was, he had no way of getting into the exclusive sector. And even if Stacia exited that space anytime soon, another woman might still be in trouble.

He didn't like the choices—lose Stacia or lose another woman.

Both were no-win situations.

He moved back into the main body of the club, looking for signs of Delgado, Pushkin or any of their associates. Hoping for something he could use to justify entering the private area in an official capacity.

They were nowhere to be found.

He spent another hour prowling through the club, on the lookout for any aberrant happenings, but there were none. There was also still no sign of Stacia; nor did he feel her presence anywhere nearby.

He slipped behind a column along the edge of the gaming part of the club. The noise was lower in this section, although the electronic pings and buzzes coupled with the shouts of the players at the assorted games presented its own challenge. He dialed his team and requested their report. Unfortunately, they advised that there had been no action in the back alley behind the club. He advised them that he was heading out to join them for a little bit, needing some fresh air to clear his mind and decide what to do next.

But even though he made that decision to regroup, something compelled him to stroll past the entrance to the private area, linger there a bit longer before he finally forced himself to go meet with Brock and Walker.

The young woman's name was Andrea.

Stacia recognized the name immediately— she was the daughter of Alex's colleague.

"Your father is looking for you. He didn't give up," she told the young woman. They were sitting side by side on the cold cement floor, waiting for something else to happen.

Andrea's brows furrowed together as she considered Stacia's statement. "Why would my father give up?"

Stacia hesitated, uncertain of how much to tell Andrea. Her reluctance surprised her since she wasn't used to emotions like compassion. But it was compassion that made her delay.

"Why would he give up?" Andrea repeated, leaning toward Stacia.

Stacia sighed and then answered, "Because there are other women missing. Women that no one has been able to find for weeks."

Andrea shook her head, slowly at first, but then the action became more vehement. "My dad *never* gave up on me, not even when I didn't deserve his trust."

Emotion welled up in Stacia once more. What would it be like to have such faith in another? To have another person care for you that deeply?

To have Alex care for her with such depth of emotion.

She embraced the young woman, understanding that was what a human might do to offer comfort. "Your dad called a friend for help. *My* friend."

She hoped she could think of Alex that way—as a friend, at least.

"Are you a cop?" Andrea asked, leaning her head against Stacia's shoulder in a gesture so trusting that it caused a hitch in the middle of Stacia's chest.

"I'm not a cop, but I can help," she answered truthfully.

A second later, the door opened and Santos tossed in another woman, who stumbled into the room before righting herself and heading to the far corner of the space. She huddled there, clearly frightened.

Arm in arm, Stacia and Andrea rose and walked over to the new occupant. Welcomed her into their embrace.

The woman wrapped her arms around them and began to cry. Whispered a heartbreaking, "I'm not alone anymore."

"No, you're not," Stacia answered.

More than any of them, Stacia knew what it was like to be alone. But unlike them, when this was all over, she would still not have anyone who cared for her in her undead life.

When this was over, she would be alone again, unless...

She drove away thoughts of Alex and all that they had shared. As much as she wanted to hope for more, she had begun to worry that it had only been a passing fancy. An aberration.

When his assignment was over, they would go their separate ways because that was the only thing Alex could ever really care about—the duty to those he protected.

Love had no place in his life, much as it had no place in hers. If she remembered that, she would avoid the pain that was sure to follow.

In the meantime, she had to continue with her plan and make sure that these woman made it home.

## Chapter 21

Alex stalked back and forth several times past the mouth of the alley, hoping with each pass that he might spot something happening.

Nothing.

Time and time again, there was no activity in the back alley, even though it had been nearly two hours since Stacia had disappeared.

He glanced at his watch and told himself the lack of any movement was to be expected. It was nearly two in the morning, early by South Beach standards. If any kind of exchange was going to happen, it would likely occur later when the area was emptier of people and traffic.

But it had to happen tonight, he thought. It was Thursday, and the next two days would be too busy for any kind of transfer. And if it didn't happen...

Orendain was going to pull the plug on the investigation on Saturday.

It had to happen tonight or else...

He wouldn't think about the "or else." Wouldn't think about what would happen to the missing women if they weren't able to stop the exchange.

But he also couldn't stop thinking about Stacia. About her safety and keeping her from harm, as well. He cared for her, no matter how often he had told himself in the past few days that it was insane to harbor such feelings for a vampire elder.

Stacia had proved herself to be a captivating mix of strength, intelligence, foolhardiness and vulnerability. A combination that called to him more than her beauty and passionate spirit.

So Alex continued to watch and worry.

When the foot traffic dwindled as the night grew older, he decided that he couldn't keep pacing along the street without attracting attention. Instead, he walked around the block and to the surveillance van parked at the far end of the alley.

Tapping on the side of the van, there was a slight delay as the team confirmed who it was, opened the rear door and then he stepped inside.

"Getting antsy?" Brock said as Alex plopped down onto a stool toward the front of the van.

"You might say that," Alex admitted.

"Don't worry. We'll get them," Walker chimed in, but pouted in clear dismay.

"Something wrong, Samantha?" he asked and accepted a cup of coffee that Brock handed him.

"If you wanted someone to go undercover—"

"I didn't. My friend decided to do that all on her own," he advised, still angry at Stacia's actions but aware there was little he could do at this point besides make sure that everything worked out well in the end.

Samantha continued with her complaint.

"Still, going undercover might have been nice—"

"Undercover work isn't nice. It's dangerous and sometimes deadly," he jumped in harshly, recalling the events of his own last covert assignment.

"Besides, you're not hot enough," Brock interjected in jest, attempting to lighten the tone.

"Bite me," Walker responded and turned toward the monitors feeding the images from the alley.

"You wish, sweet cheeks," Brock retorted, but as Alex shared a moment with the other man, it was obvious Brock wished it as well, which so totally explained the constant sniping between the two.

Alex turned his attention to the monitors and sipped on the coffee. It was lukewarm and slightly bitter, but then again the surveillance vans weren't equipped with Starbucks. Impatiently he eyeballed the action—or should he say the lack of action—going on in the alley. After about half an hour, he couldn't sit still anymore.

He gulped down the remaining bit of coffee and stood as far as the low ceiling of the van permitted. Grabbing an earpiece and transmitter from the surface of the narrow table beneath the monitors, he wired himself, wanting to be ready if they had to roll that night.

*When* they had to roll, he corrected, trying to remain optimistic that everything would work out.

Brock and Walker copied his actions, and when they were both wired, he said, "Can you hear me?"

"Roger," Walker replied, and then Brock did the same.

He had picked up their voices in his earpiece, so with a nod, he exited the van and walked back around the block.

There was decidedly less activity in front of the Widget. Only a few stragglers remained as the bouncers worked to remove the ropes they used for crowd control in preparation for closing the club for the night. Alex leaned against the wall of the building, removed a cigar and lit it. Blowing a fragrant plume of smoke, he hung out at the corner, looking like someone just enjoying the quiet late night.

But he kept a careful vigil on the building and the area around it. Seeing no hints of anything out of the ordinary. Registering no sign or sense of Stacia.

"Nothing here," he said softly, to which Walker answered back, "Nothing here, either, boss."

He curbed his impatience and his growing despair. Neither would do any good on this assignment.

It took him nearly an hour to finish the cigar, and under other circumstances it might have been a pleasurable smoke since the *puro* had been from La Gloria Cubana and exceptional. The taste of it lingered in his mouth, but he would have preferred a different flavor.

*Stacia, where the hell are you?* he wondered, knowing he couldn't hang around any longer at that spot without attracting undue attention from either the club's personnel or a passing police cruiser making its nightly rounds.

The street was virtually empty at this

point, so he walked eastward, passing the main entrance to the building. Pausing at a garbage can to fully extinguish the stub of the cigar before he tossed it in.

Then he slowly ambled across the mouth of the alley where he suddenly discerned a pair of lights turning into the narrow roadway.

"Do you copy that?" he asked his team.

"Got it. We're already working to trace the plates," Brock advised.

Alex glanced over his shoulder. A bouncer lingered at the entrance, dragging the last piece of the rope and its stanchions inside. The man caught sight of him, so Alex waved as if to say good-night, but instead of continuing eastward, he walked back toward the center of the Lincoln Road mall.

A series of intermittent gardens cut the broad width of the pedestrian plaza. He walked until there was a break in the gardens, then crossed and headed back toward the Widget. The low shrubs and palm trees offered him a clear view down the alley while disguising his presence from anyone near the club.

A panel van was driving down the narrow path between the two rows of buildings, and as it reached the midway point, the driver flashed the lights off and on several times. A moment later, a back door opened in the building directly across from the Widget and Delgado popped out.

"It's time to roll," Alex said and raced toward the entrance to the alley.

During the course of the past couple of hours, Santos had brought another three females into the room, making the cramped space even more claustrophobic.

Andrea and Stacia reassured each woman who entered, providing solace. An unaccustomed practice for Stacia. Not only had she not ever offered such comfort, she had never been the recipient.

Except for Alex. Alex had shown her kindness and tenderness, reawakening those emotions within her.

As she offered comfort, each woman provided her name and an estimate of how long she had been held captive.

To Stacia's surprise some had been in

spaces such as this small room for nearly three weeks. She understood the torment of such captivity. Cassius had kept her locked up in a room barely larger than a closet for months after she had first been turned. He had claimed it was to keep her safe and help her through the transition to being undead.

She had realized that his actions had been meant to insure his dominion over her. To mentally enslave her so he could later keep her physically imprisoned with less of a risk of rebellion.

In the year that followed after Cassius had finally given her more freedom, she had been little more than a slave in her own home. She had come to understand his actions better as he traded the blood necessary to sustain her life for an assortment of vile and debasing acts.

It had demonstrated to her how men used women. How they controlled them for their own purposes.

But Alex had understood her fears and not abused them. Had never sought dominion over her as she might have expected.

As one of the women began to fret as they

awaited their fate, Stacia reached out and took hold of her hand.

"Do not worry. You will soon be free."

"How can you be so sure?" the woman nearly wailed, almost at the limits of her restraint. She had been the one who had been imprisoned the longest and therefore had the most tenuous hold on sanity.

"Because I know there are people waiting for us. Good people who will stop these men," she asserted, the tone of her voice certain in an attempt to allay the woman's fears. She didn't add that if Alex and his team weren't there, she would take care of Santos and the others herself.

The woman was about to renew her protest when the metal of the door groaned as it swung open.

"Stay close," Stacia whispered to the women, who rose as one and huddled together, awaiting their fate.

Santos stepped into the open doorway, a large pistol in his hand. As he noted their show of unity, he smiled and said, "Now, that's a sight I like to see. All my bitches hanging together. Nice and quiet."

From behind her, Andrea pushed forward and Stacia sensed the young woman's anger rising up.

She took hold of Andrea's hand and urged her to calm down. "Easy, Andrea. We're going to be okay."

"That's right. Follow my orders and you'll all be just fine," Santos reassured them, although sneakiness rang in his words.

With a jerk of the weapon, he motioned for them to move in the direction of the hall. "Now get out of the room and walk to your left. There are stairs at the end of the hall. Wait for me there."

Stacia hung back, allowing the other women to go before her. She wanted to be last and closest to Santos so she could deal with him if needed.

When the final woman had filed out of the room, Stacia followed her, and Santos was immediately on her tail. He leaned forward and, as if aware that her obedience was feigned, warned her with, "You're too quiet, all things considered. You should be afraid, little girl."

Stacia was tempted to snap his neck right

then and there but knew she had to wait and continue to act as if she was afraid. If the men believed there was anything wrong, they might abort the transfer. Since she hoped Alex and his team were waiting for them, ready to capture the miscreants, she couldn't allow that to happen.

So she complacently plodded along behind the other women. At the stairs they all stopped as instructed and waited for Santos. He walked past her with a warning glare, up the stairs and to the metal door at the top where he gave two quick taps.

Two quick raps came in reply and then the metal doors slowly lifted open.

Santos jogged back down the few steps to the floor of the hall. "Up the stairs. Follow the instructions of the men waiting by the door to the van."

Men, she thought. How many men? Too many for Alex and his team?

*Too many for her to handle?*

The women quickly filed up the stairs as directed. As she exited into the night, she took note of the van. Two men were at its back door. One was Latino and had a pistol in his waistband. The other was quite fair, and when he issued a command to one of the girls, it was obvious that he had a thick Russian accent.

He also had a submachine gun slung across a chest padded with some kind of protection. The padding was fairly thick, Stacia surmised by the way it hid the beat of his heart from her vamp senses.

The van was idling so she assumed there was another man behind the wheel.

As Santos came up the stairs behind her and prodded her with the tip of the pistol in the middle of her back, she heard, "DEA. Drop your weapons and raise your hands."

The cavalry had just arrived, she thought with a smile.

Alex had waited until most of the women were in the van, wanting them to be out of the line of fire. His team had confirmed that there were two other men—Delgado and one of the Russians—at the back door of the van where he could not see them. They had also confirmed that they had them in their sights and had called for backup.

But Alex knew he could not wait for the additional personnel to arrive. The men were clearly ready to depart the location.

"DEA. You're surrounded. Drop your weapons," he announced and moved from the shadows in the alley, his gun trained on Santos, who whirled on him, ready to fire.

"Drop it, Santos," he urged yet again. But instead, Santos grabbed hold of Stacia, using her as a shield.

A second later, the other two men opened fire on Brock and Walker.

Alex rushed in, taking into account every detail of what was happening. Aware that the men seemed ready to die rather than be taken prisoner.

The van lurched toward him, pulling his attention away from Stacia and Santos.

The driver was going to try to make a run for it right past him.

Alex had no choice.

He stepped into the van's way and opened fire on the driver.

The windshield shattered from the on-slaught of his shots as he kept firing until the vehicle finally lurched to the right. The van plowed into the side of the building, confirming that he had hit his target.

Something whizzed by his head and he ducked down. Santos had fired at him, but missed.

Alex couldn't return fire since Stacia was still in the way.

She might be undead, but he didn't want to see her hurt in any way.

Only a second later, however, there was a blur of sudden activity as Stacia seemed to disappear before his eyes.

Unexpectedly, he now had a clear shot at Santos.

He took it.

A stunned look crossed Santos's face before he dropped to the ground, mortally wounded.

In another blast of speed, Stacia moved toward the back door of the van and climbed in with the other women.

It took Alex a too-long second of time to realize what else was happening.

His team had taken down Delgado, who lay on the floor of the alley bleeding, but the Russian was still on his feet.

The man had on body armor. Round after round hit his body, inching him back toward the van as he sought shelter from the hail of gunfire. But he never stopped firing on Brock and Walker.

Alex raced at the shooter to get close, then stopped to aim for the one shot that would take him down—a head shot.

Before Alex could fire, one of his team attempted the same thing.

The Russian's head jerked roughly to one side, and then in a slow-motion pirouette, the man turned toward the back of the van. The submachine gun in his hand continuously spewing bullets from his death grip on the trigger.

"No-o-o-o!" Alex screamed and charged forward, hoping to knock the man down before he sprayed the back of the van with a hail of gunfire.

The back of the van holding Stacia and the other women.

An errant line of bullets from the man's weapon zinged along the cement at his feet as Alex charged forward, ignoring the risk to his own safety.

As the tip of the gun neared the door of the van, Alex launched himself at the shooter.

Stacia stood at the mouth of the van's rear door, keeping an eye on the gun battle. She had been tempted to rush out and twist the remaining man's neck, but to do so would have presented a nasty question for Alex and his team to explain after the fact.

It would have also put her in the line of fire.

A vampire could sustain some gunshot damage, but too much, or even a shot in the right organ, and she could bleed out much like a human.

So she stayed in the van, positioning the other women behind her in an effort to keep them safe.

As the gunfight continued, she reached out and grabbed hold of one of the doors, pulled it shut to offer them more protection from the bullets flying around the alley. She was about to grab the other door when she observed the gunman's movement.

He was still firing, his finger tight on the

trigger in a death reflex as he pivoted in the direction of the van.

She heard Alex's scream a second before the man completed his turn and rained a hail of gunfire on the back of the vehicle.

She held her ground at the door, unable to close it in time. Unwilling to allow the bullets to pass by her and injure any of the women within.

Duty before self, she thought, channeling Alex's strict code.

She didn't even really feel the impact of the gunshots.

It was like a series of short, sharp jabs to a body capable of withstanding punishment beyond that of a human.

She looked down and the blossoms of blood registered for only a moment before her knees crumpled and she fell out of the back of the van.

The impact with the ground dazed her.

She must already be weak from the bullet wounds. So weak she couldn't rise or turn onto her back.

Too weak, it occurred to her with greater

surprise. Stacia didn't recall ever being this debilitated.

Alex's gentle touch came at her shoulder as he gingerly eased her onto her back.

She met his stunned gaze and softly said, "It's okay."

Only it wasn't, she realized, as icy tendrils erupted in her center and slowly snaked outward.

She was dying.

The wounds were too much for the vampire to heal due to the rapid blood loss. The only way to possibly survive would be to feed, only…

A man and woman appeared behind Alex as he grasped her hand.

The woman was calling someone on a radio, requesting an ambulance.

Alex leaned close and whispered in her ear, "Don't leave me, *querida.*"

She managed to reach up with her hand, kept him close as she gathered enough energy to send him her request.

*I need to feed.*

Suddenly Alex was lifting her in his arms and cradling her tight to his chest.

"Where are you going?" the woman with the radio asked.

"She'll die before the ambulance gets here. It'll be faster if I take her in my car to the hospital. Secure the scene. When the backup arrives, process all the evidence and witnesses. I'll be back as soon as I can," he rattled off and was immediately on the move.

Stacia laid her hand on his chest, directly above his heart. Focused on the strong beat while her own heartbeat stuttered and failed as her undead life fled her body.

"You're cold," he said and pulled her snugly against him.

"Dying," she said again, before she added, "sorry."

One-word sentences were all she was capable of, and even they were draining her of strength.

"You will not die, damn it. Just hang on," he said, and a moment later, he was easing her into the seat of his convertible.

He ran around the front, jumped into the car and pulled away from the curb.

They were speeding from the scene, and the road was fairly empty. She once again sent him a message as her body crashed with each passing moment.

*I'm sorry. We should have had more time.*

He held out his arm and said, "We will. Feed on me."

"No," she mumbled and tried to shake her head, but it just flopped up and down on her neck as if she was a bobblehead doll.

He brought his arm up to her lips and said, "Feed, my love. I'll get you more later."

She followed the line of his arm and met his gaze as he pulled the convertible into a narrow gap between two older buildings. The space was so tight that there would be no prying eyes able to enter and see what was happening within the cab of the car.

Only his eyes could observe, and that was enough to stop her.

She didn't want to show him her demon again. She thought that she might rather die before repeating that idiocy.

Alex must have realized what she was thinking, because he said, "I don't care what you are. I just want you to live."

No doubt diminished the sincerity in his voice. No uncertainty occupied his actions as he undid the buttons on his sleeve and yanked it up, exposing his forearm to her.

She didn't dare believe he was doing it because he cared for her. It was just a case of his being too honorable to let her die if he had the ability to save her, she told herself as with the last of her fading energy she summoned the demon.

A feeble wave of warmth ebbed across her body as her fangs slowly inched down from her mouth. She took hold of his arm as it were a drumstick and sank her fangs into the bend of his arm. The vessels were easier to reach there and filled with rich blood.

He gasped at the force of her bite, the muscles of his arm tensing until the pleasure of the vampire's bite relaxed him.

Lord, but he tasted so good, she thought as she fed. Smelled even better. Desire rose in her as it did too often with a feeding, but she battled it back. She didn't want her passion to awaken his; only as she heard his groan, she realized it might be too late for such safeguards.

She drank until some strength returned,

then pulled away from him. If she took any more, he would be unable to function.

"You're still bleeding," he said, motioning to the assorted bullet wounds on her body.

"Not strong enough to heal."

"And I can't give you more just yet. I'm already feeling light-headed," he answered truthfully.

"Blood bags...hotel," she answered, and he nodded, understanding what he had to do next.

"Let's get you there and tend to your injuries."

He inched the convertible through the alley, emerging just a few blocks shy of the Park Central. From Collins he turned down a side street adjacent to the hotel and was lucky enough to find an empty spot just around the corner from the lobby entrance.

He quickly jumped out of the car, but paused by the trunk before he opened the passenger door. She realized why as he bent and wrapped a large towel around her to hide the blood all over her body.

Then he picked her up in his arms and hurried around the block and into the hotel. Her key was somewhere at the Widget, but Alex didn't bother to stop at the desk.

"I can jimmy the lock," he said, in response to her inquisitive look.

She settled against him, feeling drained yet again. The ride in the elevator seemed painfully slow but, as promised, Alex somehow managed to open the lock with little effort.

Inside the room, he gently laid her on the bed and immediately went to the minifridge where he removed two bags of blood. He returned to her bedside, handed her one of the bags before easing the beach towel away.

"I'm going to have to cut off your clothes and take care of those wounds," he said, not that it mattered about her garments. Her clothes were ruined anyway, she thought.

She sank her fangs into the first bag of blood and continued feeding as he pulled a small knife from an ankle sheath. Carefully he cut away her outfit, and when she was naked, he went to the bathroom and returned with water and towels.

"You don't have to—"

"Stop telling me what I don't have to do.

I want to do this." Using tender strokes with a damp towel, he began cleaning away the blood from her wounds, but frowned as he did so.

She understood why as she glanced at her body.

There were several gunshot wounds still bleeding, although not as badly as before. The two feedings had helped somewhat.

Two of the bullets remained buried in her—one in her shoulder and another in her abdomen. Because she was so weak, her body wasn't expelling the foreign bodies the way it normally would. If the bullets remained in her, the lead would slowly poison her blood, leading to a painful and agonizing death.

She laid her hand over his as he moved to clean the second wound. "The bullets are still in me. We need to get them out."

"All I have is this," he said, holding up the thin knife he had earlier used on her clothes.

"That'll do."

## Chapter 22

Alex nodded and determination filled his gaze, although a line of nervous sweat erupted along his upper lip. She reassured him softly, "It won't hurt. I can block the pain."

Alex examined her carefully. She was lying to protect him, but he had no choice but to do as she asked if he was to save her life.

Her undead life, and yet there was nothing undead about her blood on his hands. About the wounds marring her beautiful body.

She cupped his cheek and urged him on. "You can do it."

He controlled the quaver in his hand and

went to work on the injury in the middle of her shoulder. He palpated the wound to see how deep the bullet might be, then using the tip of the knife, he worked it in until he encountered metal. Using a combination of pressure and the knife, he extracted the bullet.

The entire time she didn't cry out, although he had seen the flinch of pain skittering across her body as he applied pressure.

When the bullet came free of her body, blood immediately welled up and out of the freshly aggravated injury. He grabbed a washcloth and applied pressure, then asked her to take his place at maintaining the tension as he tackled the second injury.

This wound was more serious as the bullet had penetrated deep into her abdomen. He wondered if vamps could develop peritonitis or other infections since they clearly could bleed to death like humans.

Even more carefully, he applied pressure to gauge the location of the wound. A soft moan escaped her this time, but she quickly reined herself in.

His hand shook as he touched the tip to

the ravaged skin of her abdomen. Slowly he penetrated inward until he once again encountered the resistance of metal. Carefully he moved the knife and found a way to gingerly bring the bullet to the surface.

The slug came out easier, but even more blood escaped this injury, and as his hand brushed her flesh, the cold, wet chill on her skin registered on his fingers.

"Stacia?" he inquired, then realized she was almost unconscious.

Applying a washcloth to the injury on which he had just labored, he picked up the blood bag with his other hand and brought it to her lips. Pressed it to her mouth and urged, "Feed, *querida*. You need to feed."

She placed her lips on the bag, fumbled with it for a moment before she seemed to find purchase on the slick surface of the plastic and bit down.

He stared in fascination as her mouth worked the bag, draining it, but when she finished, he realized it still wasn't enough. Leaving her side, he removed two more bags from the fridge—the last two.

He held a bag up to her lips, let her feed.

For the second helping, she had the strength to hold it herself.

He turned his attention to ripping the sheet into long strips so he could bind her wounds.

Tension filled her body as he carefully tended to her, a testament to the pain he had thought she couldn't feel with her vampire power. When he finished, she had drained the last bag and seemed to have a little more strength.

He covered her with a light bedspread and sat beside her, taking hold of her hand. Her skin was still slightly chilled, but the damp sweat that had bathed her before had dissipated to some degree.

"I need to go back to the crime scene," he said, dismayed that he had to leave her but having little choice.

"I know. I'll be okay." Surprising frailness filled her voice.

"I'll be back."

"There's no need—"

"I'll be back," he said, stronger this time to reinforce his conviction.

She nodded and closed her eyes. As he rose, he thought he detected a hint of tears escaping her eyelids. It tore at his heart, threatening common sense. Yet, as he had said, he had no choice.

Duty called, and for the moment it took precedence over the demands of his heart.

He returned to the alley to find that Brock was overseeing the processing of the crime scene while a duo of Miami Beach Police Department cruisers were keeping away prying eyes. He approached Brock, and one of the officers stepped into his way, but he pulled out his badge and flashed it at the man. The police officer stepped to the side and Alex hurried to where Brock stood.

"What's the status?" Alex asked.

Brock motioned to the DEA officers working the scene, taking pictures and collecting evidence. The driver of the van was dead at the wheel. The Russian who had fired on Stacia and the women lay sprawled by the back of the van.

"Three dead. Santos and both Russians, but neither of them is Pushkin. Orendain got a warrant to search the ship for him and is on his way with two other agents. Delgado is alive and at the hospital," Brock replied, then motioned to the police officers.

"Miami Beach P.D. came by to take the women to the hospital. No injuries from the gunfire, but we wanted to make sure they were physically sound after their imprisonment. Walker went with them and will be taking their initial statements before we notify the families."

"Was one of them Andrea McAnn?" he asked, saying a silent prayer beneath his breath.

"She was. We haven't called Dan yet. Figured you'd want to do that."

He slapped Brock on the back. "Thanks. You and Walker did a great job."

Brock smiled and nodded, but then his face became serious. "How's your friend who was shot?"

"She's hanging tough. If you don't need me anymore—"

"Go ahead. We've got this under control here. Besides, you know Orendain is going to make sure to be here to meet the press." Brock released an exasperated sigh as he added, "That man hogs all the glory."

"There are lots of things more important than the glory." Alex clapped Brock on the back again and left, eager to return to Stacia and make sure she was getting better.

He got back into his convertible, but before returning to the hotel, he dialed Dan McAnn.

Dan answered with a sleepy "Hello."

"Dan, it's Alex. I've got some good news for you," he said, and Dan's voice immediately brightened.

"You found Andrea," he said, and a woman's voice echoed the statement in the background. Andrea's mom, he assumed.

"We did. She's okay but at Jackson Memorial just to be on the safe side. Agent Walker is with her and will be calling you a little later."

"Oh, my God, Alex. I don't know what to say. I can't thank you enough," Dan replied, his voice shaking with emotion.

"No need, Dan. You would have done it for me."

"Seriously, Alex. Whatever you need—"

"Actually, I need to go. I've got an injured witness I need to visit," he replied, itching to return to Stacia.

"I understand. Good night, Alex, and thanks again."

"Good night." He snapped the cell phone shut, tossed it onto the passenger seat and pulled away from the curb. In the early-morning hours, there was little traffic, and Alex made it back to the hotel in just a few minutes.

*Stacia,* he thought with longing and hurried in, wasting barely any time before he was standing beside her bed.

Her breathing barely stirred the light bedspread with which he had covered her. She was pale, but was she more pallid than before? he wondered as he sat beside her and cupped her cheek.

It seemed even colder than when he had left, but she gradually regained consciousness.

"You came back," she said, so softly he almost didn't hear her.

He ran the pad of his thumb across her cheek. "You're chilled."

Stacia nodded, battling the urge to slip back to sleep. Dawn was coming, but she was so drained she feared that if she allowed herself the rest, she would never rise again. Another feeding might help, only...

"What can I do?" he asked, but she just gave another wobbly shake of her head, unable to ask for what she needed most from him.

He undid the buttons on his bloodstained shirt and tossed it aside, offered her his arm once again, but she refused.

"I can't," she replied.

"Why? You need to feed, Stacia. You're still too weak."

"I'll be fine," she said, but he saw it for the lie that it was.

"Why are you doing this? Why did you risk your life tonight?" he pressed.

In the short time he had been away, she had been asking herself the same thing. Wondering why the lives of those women had mattered so much. Maybe even more than her own.

Why she would risk her own immortal existence, but deep in her heart she knew why.

"I thought my humanity was gone. That I couldn't care anymore about anyone else," she replied.

His brows furrowed together as he contemplated her response, but then he said, "You did it to prove your humanity? That you could still feel compassion?"

Compassion and more, she thought. She had needed to prove to herself that she could feel that and more. That she could still experience love, because in the short time they had been together, he had touched something deep within her. Brought a piece of her back to life.

Only, now the dawn was coming and threatening to take it all away.

She shot a worried glance at the window, where the first rays of sunlight were leaking past the edges of the blackout curtains. And because these might be her last conscious minutes, she locked her gaze on his and confessed her secret.

"Humanity. Compassion. Love. I needed to know I could still love."

Shock registered in his eyes, but what came next surprised her even more. A sad smile played across his lips as he said, "I know you can love. I've felt it when we're together because I feel the same way. I love you."

She didn't want to believe. Especially not now when she stood at death's door, but then he offered his arm to her again.

"*Por favor,* Stacia. Humanity is about what's in your heart. Not about hiding the demon."

His words tore something free inside, lightening her spirit. But she had to be honest with him about what he was ready to bestow on her. "Each bite will bind us closer. The connection between us—"

"Is one that I want, *querida.* I'm not afraid of what's happening between us. Not anymore."

When he offered his arm yet again, she dared to believe but wanted to gift him with more. "Not like that, *mi amor.* Let me share myself with you."

He smiled and said, "With pleasure and love."

His words dragged a smile to her face. She watched as he finished undressing and then slipped beneath the covers with her. As he brought his body close, she snuggled to the warmth of it and murmured, "You feel good."

He ran his hand lightly over the wounds he had bandaged. "Are they…better?"

"They're not yet healed, but once I feed… they'll get better," she said and laid her hand over the spot on his chest above his heart. Spreading her fingers, her palm pressed to feel the beat of it, she touched the edge of his scar with her pinkie. As she moved upward to bring her mouth to the edge of his neck and shoulder, tension crept into his body.

She tried to ease his discomfort. "It won't hurt as much as this did," she said and traced the edges of the scar with her finger.

"As long as it'll keep you with me." He wrapped an arm around her waist and closed the distance between them.

She gripped his upper arm with one hand while the other remained pressed between their bodies, close to his heart and the scar of his old wound. As she brought her mouth toward the fragile skin at the side of his neck, she whispered, "As much as I want you with me forever, I won't turn you, *mi amor*. Do not fear."

He brushed his lips across hers. "I'm not afraid of the demon."

But something else was troubling him. Stacia could sense it and wanted him to understand. "I'm not like Diana. I won't love you and then leave."

Somehow Alex had known that. Had recognized that when Stacia fell in love, it was a forever kind of thing. A human's forever, he thought, recalling her promise about not making him a vampire. Slipping another kiss across her lips, he said, "I love you."

"I love you, too, Alex. More than I ever could have dreamed possible," she said, but her words were slightly slurred, and as he met her gaze, it occurred to him that the call of dawn was pulling her away from him.

"Feed. Now, before it's too late," he said and urged her mouth to his neck.

A second later the sharp points of her fangs grazed his skin. He braced himself and her breath spilled along his skin a heartbeat before the sting came.

It did hurt less than being shot, he thought, focusing on the feel of her lips on his skin. On their tug and pull, which yanked at him, calling forth passion. Arousing ardor in a slow, steady pulse until his need was so great that he cried out her name.

"Stacia."

She moaned and eased her one hand down to encircle him. Tenderly she explored the length of him as she continued to feed, and passion steadily rose in his body until it almost consumed him.

As a guttural sound of pleasure/pain escaped his lips, Stacia finally pulled away from the temptation of his blood.

She was breathing heavily, and as their gazes collided, the blue-green glow of the vampire met his.

"What is this?" he asked, cradling her back in his hands as she continued to caress him.

"The vampire's kiss can bring great pleasure," she explained.

Pleasure so great he was nearly dizzy from it, and yet, it would be empty pleasure if he couldn't share it with her. But he sensed she was still weak, and with a long inhalation, he pushed back his need.

Beneath her hand, his erection jerked for a moment before beginning to soften. Confusion overtook her before he said, "I want it to be with you, but when you're better. Rest now. We have forever."

*Forever,* she thought and allowed herself to believe in that possibility. His blood, so rich and full of life, had helped to restore her life energy. Although the rising sun continued to draw her to slumber, this time she thought she had enough strength to rouse from that sleep.

As her eyelids drooped, she battled the drowsiness long enough to say, "I love you, Alex. You've brought me back to life."

And not just with his blood, she thought as his arms embraced her and sleep pulled her away from him.

His love had reanimated her soul. Awakened real passion, which had been missing from her life for too long.

His lips brushed her temple as she snuggled against his warmth, knowing that he would be there when she woke.

## Chapter 23

The warmth and weight of his body were a welcome change to the many times she had woken alone. Her eyelids fluttered open and then her gaze locked on his—her human gaze, filled with appreciation and love.

"How are you?" he asked while tenderly stroking the line of her jaw with his thumb.

"Much better."

Alex gestured to the makeshift bandage he had made for the wound on her shoulder. "Can I check?"

Stacia nodded and Alex slipped from the bed. He removed his knife from the ankle sheath lying on the floor and carefully used it to cut away the strips of sheet binding her shoulder. He removed the piece of towel he had used to apply pressure to the wound. Where yesterday there had been a gaping gunshot wound, now there was just smooth, creamy skin.

He repeated the process at the three other wound sites. Each had healed shut without a mark to signal that she had been injured.

Smiling, he gathered up all the dirty bandages and tossed them in the trash before returning to her side.

"All better," she said as he gazed down at her.

He reached up and touched the spot on his neck where she had fed. "Me, too."

She sat up but wavered, and he grasped her arms to steady her.

"Still a trifle weak," she admitted, which surprised him. He suspected she wasn't used to such confessions.

"Would it help—"

"How about a bath before that? It would be nice to be clean of the stench of the blood."

Interesting, he thought. But then again, he

wouldn't like walking around wearing half his dinner, either. Not to mention that traces of blood lingered on his body from the events of the night before.

"A bath. I'll get it going."

She shot him a grateful smile and leaned back against the pillows, clearly not yet fully restored.

He brushed a kiss across her lips before he left and hurried to the bathroom where he turned on the water to fill the large claw-foot tub. He spilled in some of the bath salts sitting on a filigreed stand beside the bath.

Within seconds the aromas permeated the air—eucalyptus and, beneath it, something citrusy if he had to guess.

He placed a washcloth and two towels within easy reach, and when the tub was two-thirds full, he returned to the bedroom.

She still rested in bed but had pulled the light bedspread back over her body.

"Cold?" he asked, and she nodded.

"A little."

He remembered how she had felt the night before, frigid as ice and covered with a scary, sickly sweat. He had to know. "Is it because of the vampire?"

Stacia shook her head. "The transformation to the vampire brings warmth. The cold and chill is when I'm in my human state or when true death is near."

True death.

Recalling her injuries, he knew just how close she had come to leaving him.

"Don't risk your life like that again," he said softly.

She sat up then and the bedspread dropped from her body, revealing her to him. Stroking her fingers across the scar on his chest and then down across the one on his abdomen, she said, "Can I ask you to do the same?"

Because he wasn't sure he could make a similar promise, he decided to change the subject. "The bath's ready."

Stacia recognized his ploy but understood the reason for it. Risking his life was part of what he felt he had to do for the greater good, but she hadn't lived as long as she had by thinking of others. And last night, when she had, look at where it had gotten her.

Back in his arms, she thought as he lifted

her from the bed and walked to the bathroom. At the edge of the tub, he slowly let her slip down into the water.

"Soak for a bit. I'm going to clean up the other room."

He left and she leaned her back against the high edge of the tub and allowed the heat to permeate her undead body. From the other room, she heard the noise as he worked. The bed shifting and the zip of linens coming off the mattress. The rustle of new sheets and the groan of wood on wood as he moved the bed back into place.

When he returned, he paused by the side of the tub and gazed down at her. His body was tense, and between his legs, his penis stirred and slowly rose to attention.

She understood. He was a man, after all, and attracted to her. Heat erupted between her legs as she imagined him sliding within her, but as she did so, the warmth of the vampire grew inside, reminding her of other needs she still had to fulfill.

Even with that knowledge, she wanted him, but not in haste.

Reaching up, she ran her hand along his

erection, spreading the warm water on her palm on his sensitive skin. Stroking him tenderly and experiencing the swell and shift of him beneath her hand.

"Stacia," he half warned, because she knew he didn't really want her to stop touching him.

"Come and join with me," she said, sitting up even farther to give him the room to step into the tub.

He did so, sitting opposite her. His knees drawn up slightly because of the size of the tub, creating a barrier between them until she slipped over his legs and laid her body along the length of his.

He groaned, but her cry joined his as she relished the warm strength of his body along hers. Coveting the hard proof of his desire beneath her belly. Needing it so badly that she shifted upward so she could guide him into her.

"Stacia, are you sure?" he asked, but she gave him her answer with the motion of her hips as she sat on him, taking him deeply into her body.

Their mutual gasps filled the air, but then

silence came as she rested flush against his body, wanting to experience every inch of him.

Alex nearly came from the feel of her surrounding him.

Somehow he controlled it and wrapped his arms around her as she lay along him, their bodies joined together from toe to chest. He stroked the line of her back with one hand while keeping her resting on him with the other.

"That feels good," she murmured against his chest and then dropped a kiss at a spot just above his heart. Swept her hand across his pectoral muscle and the hard brown nub at its center.

It did feel good. Being inside of her while she leisurely touched him was an amazing experience. Feeling her skin beneath his hand, so soft and slick from the water. The hard points of her breasts pressed into his chest, and he reached around and stroked the back of his hand against the tip.

At her murmur of approval, he deepened his caress, rotating the nub between his thumb and forefinger, drawing a pleased sigh from her.

She sat up, granting him access to her breasts, but also deepening his penetration with the shift of her hips.

This time he moaned, but she teasingly said, "Time to wash."

Grasping the washcloth he had left within easy reach, she drenched it in the water and then applied some bath gel. Worked the gel into a fluffy lather that she spread across his chest and arms. Following the path of the washcloth in one hand with the brush of the palm of her other hand.

When her roving hands passed across his sensitive paps, his balls tightened and he nearly came from her leisurely exploration, but he sucked in a breath and contained himself.

"Did you like that?" she asked and once again ran the washcloth and her hands across his chest, pausing at his nipples to tweak them.

He groaned and jerked beneath her, barely retaining control.

"It's okay to come, Alex. I promise we

will share more later," she said, and after, she cupped her hands to splash warm water across his chest, rinsing it of the soap.

Before he could register her intent, she bent her head and licked the tip of one hard nipple.

He moaned and cupped her head to him. As she teased the tip of him with her teeth, she lifted her hips slightly. The warmth of the water replaced her more intense heat, but then she eased back over him and that simple friction was enough to send him over the edge.

He called her name as he shuddered, lost in the sensation of her body and touch.

She shifted on him again, prolonging the pleasure of his climax. The friction working him, milking his seed deep into her. Deep into a place where no life would take hold.

Sadness filled him then and she must have sensed it.

She lifted her gaze and her eyes gleamed with tears she would not shed.

"Of all the emotions I want from you, pity isn't on the list."

Never pity, he thought, realizing that she

had accepted the existence given to her when her human life had been taken. Shown strength beyond that of most.

"Will you take love, instead?" he asked, because he could freely acknowledge what his heart had been telling him from the first time he had laid his eyes on her.

A bittersweet smile crept onto her lips and the tears that finally slipped from her eyes were tears of joy.

"I will."

He kissed her then, delighting in the sweetness of her kiss, tinged as it were with the salt of her happiness.

Over and over they kissed, until they were both breathing heavily and his erection had come back to life within her.

He felt a chill on her skin. Knew there was something not quite right.

"Stacia. Are you okay?"

She released a tired sigh. "I'm just a little shaky."

"Will it help if you—"

She covered his lips with her hand. "I warned you earlier that each bite—"

"Binds us closer, but we are already close,"

he said, and to prove the point, he surged upward with his hips.

She was not convinced by his actions, although his movement dragged her eyes shut for a moment as passion swept over her.

When her gaze returned to him, the edges of her irises were tinged with the blue-green of the vampire.

"Do not mistake physical ties with those of the mind—"

"And heart," he said, covering the spot between her breasts and right above her heart with his hand.

"You said you were sure before, but—"

"I'm sure now. If you ask me again tonight or tomorrow, I'll still be as certain—I love you."

Within her heart, hope renewed itself and Stacia allowed herself to believe. To once again accept the gifts he was bestowing.

"And I you. I've never met a man more honorable or loving," she acknowledged.

"Now that that's settled…"

He ran his hand along the line of her collarbone and then up to cradle the back of her head. Sitting up, he urged her closer, anxious as he waited for her bite. Tense until she whispered against the shell of his ear, "Relax. Allow the call of my ardor into your body."

Following her words, a wave of energy swelled over him and renewed desire in his body.

As he wrapped his arms around her, dragging her near until every inch of their bodies was in contact, her fangs grazed the skin at his neck.

He shook, but not from fear.

As she sank her teeth into him, her ardor swept over him, filling his body with immense pleasure. Desire made more intense by the love that bound them.

Her lips moved against his skin as she fed, but she also shifted her hips, riding him. The friction of her body stroking him, slowly building toward a climax.

He was on the edge, nearly at his peak when she ripped away from him.

By the time he met her gaze, she had returned to her human state. The passion of the vampire ebbed but was quickly replaced by the sweetness of her hips moving on his. By the feel of her mouth and tongue renewing their earlier kiss.

The water lapped around them as they continued making love until with one last upward thrust into her welcoming depths, he heard her cry of release.

Alex finally allowed himself to come then, holding her hips to bury himself deep where she milked him with her body until he was spent.

Arms wrapped around each other, they lingered in the bathwater for just a few more minutes as it was losing its warmth. They broke apart only long enough to towel down and then were immediately in each other's arms again, moving toward the clean bed Alex had prepared earlier.

They fell onto the sheets and each other, making love yet again before resting for a few hours, spooned together beneath the covers.

But as they lay there, he sensed unease creeping into her body and wanted to quash it.

"What's wrong?" he asked, grasping her hand when she would have pulled away from him.

"I don't know what to think about this... about us," she said.

"You're not sure about what this is?"

With a careless shrug, she replied, "I'm scared this is not for real."

"What would it take to make you stop doubting? If you turned me—"

She covered his lips with her free hand. "I don't want to make you like I am."

Alex kissed the palm of her hand and then covered it with his, urged her close with a gentle tug. "Like you? You say that as if it's a bad thing."

"I've done bad things," she reminded him, almost as if she wanted to push him away.

"We've all done bad things." To prove his point, he covered her mouth with his and kissed her hungrily, wanting to drive away any of her remaining hesitation with the wonder of what they could experience together.

She answered his kiss and heat built quickly within him, almost like a flash fire. In his brain he heard, "It's because of the bond."

He moved away, but barely. The spill of her nearly nonexistent breath fell across his lips as she said, "You make me feel things I shouldn't."

"Like?" he questioned and began to kiss her once again.

"Hope," she said. In between kisses, she added, "Love. Happiness."

"Such bad, bad things," he teased, drawing a confused chuckle from her.

"You're not going to go away, are you?"

He turned serious then, certain of one thing. "I won't go away. I love you too much to just walk away from this."

Stacia's smile this time was bright and unrestrained.

"I guess that makes two of us," she said.

Alex didn't delay. Pulling her close, he brought his mouth to the gap between her neck and shoulder, gently biting her.

Stacia moaned and held his head to her, delicious need building in her as he sucked at the spot. When he finally moved away, he dragged a finger across where he had marked her and it sent a zing of pleasure rocketing through her body, yanking a guttural cry from her.

As his gaze met hers, puzzlement filled hers until he said, "With each bite—"

"The connection grows stronger," she finished for him and smiled.

"Seems only fair that it works both ways, don't you think," he said and once again stroked the tender spot at her neck.

Stacia brought her lips to his, whispered against them, "You are bold, *mi amor.*"

"And you love that. Love me," he said.

Her smile broadened beneath his lips as she said, "I love you, Alex. You've made me feel alive again."

As he kissed her, accepting the gift of her love, he realized what a twisted path love had taken before uniting them. But as he made love with her, he knew the road they would travel in the future would be smoother because together they were stronger than they were alone.

*Love makes all things possible,* he thought before giving himself over to her Stacia and her immortal devotion.

\* \* \* \* \*

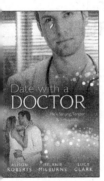
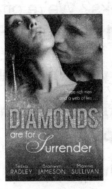
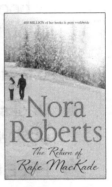